GORILLA CARGO: THE COMPLETE
ADVENTURES OF McNALLY, VOLUME 1

BOOKS IN THE ARGOSY LIBRARY:

GOLDEN RIVER: THE COMPLETE
ADVENTURES OF BEN QUORN, VOLUME 1
TALBOT MUNDY

LADY OF THE NIGHT WIND
VARICK VANARDY

KING OF THE EXILES
THOMSON BURTIS

FOR A POINT OF HONOR: THE COMPLETE
CASES OF RIORDAN, VOLUME 2
VICTOR MAXWELL

THE DARK WATERS
WILLIAM CORCORAN

MURDER WITHOUT MOTIVE: THE COMPLETE
CASES OF SHOW-ME McGEE, VOLUME 1
FREDERICK C. DAVIS

MURDER IN THE NUDIST CLUB
FRED MACISAAC

GORILLA CARGO: THE COMPLETE
ADVENTURES OF McNALLY, VOLUME 1
RICHARD WORMSER

GREEN MAMBA: THE COMPLETE
CASES OF DAFFY DILL, VOLUME 2
RICHARD B. SALE

THE SILENCER MYSTERY: THE COMPLETE
CASES OF GILLIAN HAZELTINE, VOLUME 3
GEORGE F. WORTS

GORILLA CARGO
THE COMPLETE ADVENTURES
OF McNALLY, VOLUME 1

RICHARD WORMSER

ILLUSTRATED BY
SAMUEL CAHAN

COVER BY
EMMETT WATSON

POPULAR PUBLICATIONS · 2024

TABLE OF CONTENTS

SNAKE CHARMER

*Bullets from phantom guns, a rotting inn
and a girl with frightened eyes—these
things Dave McNally found when he went
hunting snakes in that Florida swamp*

1

REPTILES WANTED

DAVE MCNALLY SAT with his feet on his roll-topped desk and languidly cleaned a gun. He was neither gangster, private detective nor sportsman; the gun would certainly not have suited either of the first two classes of marksmen, and few sportsmen have ever handled an electric elephant rifle.

Below his window Times Square rattled and roared, with the clamor of a million people trying to make a dime, and another million trying to spend one. The sun was going down behind the Hudson, and enough of its rays came through the canyons of the Forties to shine in Dave's gray eyes. He turned his swivel chair so as to face the other way. Now he was confronted with the hieroglyphics that are the backward for:

D.N. McNALLY

Expeditions & Amusements

A shadow bulked behind the plate glass background for this message, and the door opened.

"Don't shoot," the newcomer said. "I'll come down."

McNally laid down the rifle and swung to his feet. He gazed down at the visitor with something like amusement

The snake coiled to spring

in his face. "Hiyah, Jake. I thought the McLaren Carnival was playing the cornbelt."

Jake McLaren sighed, sitting down. "The cornbelt's playing it," he said. "You seen the reports? Some weeks we almost make enough to buy wood for the cook tent, if we had any food to cook. I'm running the sideshow for a concession out at the island."

"Yeah? How's that going?"

"Not so good, Dave, or I wouldn't be here," Jake McLaren said sadly. "What with midget villages and such, the competish's too high. Know where we can pick up one good freak?"

"Nothing that isn't being used some place on the Midway already."

Jake McLaren got down to cases. He pulled up his trousers over his fat knees, rested his hands on his haunches and leaned over. "Dave," he said, "the gun what runs this show has dough. Real dough, and he'll sink it all to make the concesh pay out. Now, I can get Steffa Ninksa, you know, the snake charmer. She's got the class and the looks—only she ain't got the snakes. I want you should get us the two largest snakes in captivity, only the largest, what I mean."

McNally laughed. "For a minute I thought you meant business, Jake. But snakes, you can wire to Florida, get snakes for two bucks apiece. Large as Steffo will handle 'em."

"No, Dave, you can't. See, we really mean snakes. Now, down in a swamp behind St. Michael City, when I was down there last winter, I heard about real snakes. Only none of the natives would go get 'em for me. Big fellas, twelve feet long and more, and thick as Steffa herself."

Dave looked interested. "Natives wouldn't get 'em, huh? That's funny. Those Florida crackers down there pride themselves on going up against anything, Jake. How come?"

Jake looked apologetic. "Well, you would laugh at me, Dave, only I got the money to put on the line. They say there are ghosts in that swamp. See, I knew you'd laugh, only—I want those snakes. The swamp's only a couple of miles long, by about a mile wide. You can cover it in two days."

The fat man reached into his pocket, brought out a wallet. At the sight of the money, Dave McNally began to grin. He flicked a hand towards the door. "O.K.," he said. "You see the sign. Expeditions & Amusements. This sounds like more of an amusement than an expedition, Jake, but it's your money." He reached for a time table. "Where is this place?"

"Rawley Acres, just outside of St. Michael City," Jake said. "This Rawley was a real estate guy, like they had in Florida during the boom. Since he went broke, the thing's gone back to the swamps."

Dave McNally wrote it down....

THE TAXI DRIVER said: "There's Rawley Acres we's running along now." He jerked a hand over the edge of the wheel. Off into the palmetto scrub and jackpine ran concrete pavements, each a half a city block long; their edges were covered over by sand and weeds, their ends were no place. "Peck of money been lost in thet swamp," the taxi driver added, cheerfully. "Yes, sir, some fella with not much on his mind, he figgered out one day every 'gator in that swamp's worth five thousand dollars. Gave old man Rawley half a 'gator myself, back when he was promoting."

Dave McNally studied the swamps that began just back of those futile pavements. "What happened to Rawley?"

"Got on a boat to go up to N'Yawk to study with a bond-holders' committee. Boat got there, but Rawley didn't."

"Jumped or fell, eh?"

"Reckon so. He'd a hundred thousand dollars' wuth of insurance, some say a million. His wife took it, she travels to Europe now all the time. Raickon she couldn't face all the folks round here lost money." He turned the car off the road. "Yon's the beach, mister. Really almost an island, I guess, 'tween the acres and the ocean. You aimin' to sell somethin' out yeah?"

"I'm staying a few days," McNally said. "There's a hotel, isn't there?"

"Yes, sir, that there is." The taxi driver seemed amused. "Sure is. Minus only a roof, and mebbe a wall or two. Reckon I'll have to lug you back to town again, but it won't cost you nothin', mister."

"I'll make out all right," Dave said. "I'll only be here a day or so. There are some people living here, aren't there?"

"Yeah, some families on the beach, squatters like. You wouldn't want to sell them nothin', though. No money."

"I'm not selling anything."

The driver slowed down over the rutty, half shell road.

"No? Well, mister, there's your hotel. Guess we can start back now."

Dave McNally looked. It was a big place; but tropical wind and sand had taken half the roof off; palmetto scrub and beach grass had ruined the landscaped garden; the wreck of an old sofa had been used to replace a broken front step. Rusty metal strewed the porch.

Only smoke from a lean-to at one end proved that it had not been abandoned.

The driver watched Dave McNally quizzically.

"All right," Dave said. "Let's get the bags out. I'm staying."

The taxi driver pulled out Dave's suitcases, his hunting bags, piled them on the broken sofa. "Sure you know what you're doin', young man? You ain't sellin' nothin', ain't visitin' kinfolk; seems like a moughty funny place for a rest."

"Here, I owe you a dollar," Dave said. "I'm down here hunting snakes," he added.

The driver's face froze. "It's all right with me," he said levelly. "I'm not one to be a bad loser. Only, there's folks around here ain't never forgot how to run a lynchin' party." He kicked the car into gear with a heavy foot on the clutch pedal, and nearly went over Dave's toes. "Snake hunter," he muttered contemptuously as the car scudded away down the road.

DAVE LOOKED AROUND. Down the beach, nearly hidden by the sand dunes, three or four little shacks nestled; there was smoke coming from the top of one. Behind him lay the swamps, their lush foliage waving over more sand dunes; and ahead, between him and the surfy beach, was the hotel.

He picked up his bags, leaped over the rear end of a car,

lying half buried in the sand, and started up the hotel steps. The first step cracked under him and his foot went through, scraping the skin off his ankle.

He swore mildly and considered the next move. To walk up the steps was obviously unsafe; on the other hand, to get up by jumping would be worse, because the porch looked as though it would surely give way if anyone jumped on it.

He finally worked out the problem; the sand had piled up on one end of the hotel and he would go around there and make his entrance. He fastened the rifle over his shoulder in its canvas ease, and took a firm grip on the bags. As he walked, the soft sand gave way under him and filled his shoes, made the scrape on his ankle sting.

When he rounded the corner of the hotel, something went *plunk* into the soft wood, and a splinter stung his cheek.

It was a bullet. The noise of the shot had evidently been drowned out by the booming of the surf.

Dave McNally dropped his bags, and dropped himself too, to lie down behind them. He quickly unfastened the canvas cover, slid out his rifle, assembled it. It was a big bore Mannlicher, brought along for 'gators; it ought to be able to take on whoever had shot at him.

But there was nothing to be seen but the soft waving of the salt hay on the dunes. Dave shoved the bags aside, and lay for a moment in full view. When there was no further shot, he went forward, crouched over and running, and flung himself down behind a wrinkle in the sand. Five inches from his nose a fiddler crab dove for its hole; a little farther on, a chameleon stared at him unblinkingly, then scuttled away.

HE GOT HIS knees under him and grasped the rifle, then ran for a small dune. While he was still moving, a puff of smoke came up from behind a dune, and sand spurted behind him. This time he thought he heard the crack of a rifle.

He lay still, staring at the top of the dune from which the shot had come. Whoever had shot had evidently dropped back without waiting to see if he had hit anything. With that kind of shooting, a man ought to be able to get right up on the hidden gun worker and smoke him out. Dave began to think up things to say to the law about self-defense. Or was there any law on Rawley Acres?

The grass on the top of the dune moved suspiciously. Whoever the man was up there, he was coming up for another shot. Dave watched him through his telescopic sight.

A voice behind him said, coolly, "It is out of season for ducks."

Dave looked over his shoulder. A pair of legs that ended in beach shoes at one end and culottes at the other; a short sleeved cotton jersey; a head of bobbed hair. He let go of the rifle, rolled over, grabbed the ankles above the beach sandals, and jerked.

The girl went over hard, and landed on top of him. He shoved her off, held her down with an elbow, and muttered: "Lie still. There's someone shooting at me from up on that dune."

The girl wriggled free and stood up, brushing the sand off her. "Don't be ridiculous," she said. "There's no one there." She walked ahead of him, right along the line of his rifle barrel; there was nothing to do but get up and go with her. But Dave kept the rifle cuddled in his arms at the alert.

"My name is Virginia Rawley," the girl said. "I own the hotel back there." It was an obvious request for Dave McNally's name and business. He gave her the first, and added: "I'm hunting snakes for a sideshow. I hear there are some beauties in the swamps here."

The girl didn't bother to answer that. They were at the foot of the dune now; Dave raised the rifle, and yelled: "Stand up. I'm coming after you."

There was no answer.

"Isn't that rather childish?" Virginia Rawley said, and walked up to the top of the dune. "You see? There is no one up here."

Dave went up after her, pointed. "See? Someone was lying in the sand there. And the salt grass is pressed down there, where he walked on it to keep from leaving footprints."

"I don't see a thing," the girt said. She turned on her heel and started back for the hotel.

Dave McNally looked at her quizzically, and then followed her back again.

But he did not much care for the idea of turning his back on the dune.

2

CLOSED DOORS

HE CAUGHT UP with her at the spot where he had dropped his bags. "Is this your hotel, Miss Rawley?" he asked.

"I rent it. Yes."

"That's fine. I don't reckon I'll be here more than two or three days; just long enough to round up some natives, and go through the swamps. If these snakes are as big as I think they are, they ought to be easy to find."

"I'm sorry. The hotel doesn't take guests."

Dave grinned at her, picked up his bags, and shoved past her through a door. He was in a kitchen; he set the bags down there, walked through another door. He was now in what had been the main ballroom of the hotel; it was in much better repair than the outside would have led him to believe. In back of the front entrance there was a room that had obviously been the office.

He dug under broken chairs, three-legged tables, a gutted sofa to find what he was looking for—a copy of the hotel license. It was many years out of date.

He carried it back to the girl. His lips were pressed down tight over his teeth. "Look," he said. "This is a licensed hotel. You can't refuse to take me in."

"That thing is ten years old," the girl said.

"But you are not the owner," Dave pointed out. "You can't do anything to destroy his property rights. Once you refuse to take in guests, you prevent his ever taking out another—"

He was having such a fine time with his ridiculous argument that he did not notice what the girl was doing. She had moved around behind him, and something round and hard suddenly pressed into him. From a rifle length behind him the Rawley girl said: "Pick up your bags and get out of here."

He raised his hands and slowly turned around to face her. She was holding his Mannlicher, pointed at his midriff, and her hands were not shaking. "You heard me, snake hunter," she said. "This is my home. Please leave."

His face got cold and hard, and he bent over and picked up his two bags. He said, clearly: "I could swing this one bag into the rifle barrel and the other into your face, and knock you for a loop before the bullet could get up the barrel."

"But you're not going to," she said, "or you wouldn't have told me."

"No," he said, "I'm not. I've nothing to gain by it; I wouldn't sleep in your hotel anyway. But," he said, walking down the side porch and starting over the sand, "I never knew a girl to go to so much trouble for a pair of snakes. They must be pets of yours," he added, for no reason at all. "Or relatives."

The change in her voice was so marked that it brought him around on his heel. "Get out of here!" she shrieked. Her face was white and drawn. "Out of here, will you? Are you crazy?"

"No," Dave said. "But one of us is. So long, pal. Can I have my rifle back?"

She didn't answer. But her nerves were so obviously taut that he walked away. There was always the danger that her hands would shake, and the trigger jerk back. He still did not believe she had ever meant to shoot him.

HE FOUND A path towards the shacks he had seen. Sitting on a fallen palmetto, he took off his shoes, shook the sand out of them. He found himself moved to an unusual extent; there was something indescribably horrible about a girl who was so young, pretty and well educated, and who had in some way been worked into a position where she would threaten to shoot any stranger who came near her.

Barnum knew that Dave McNally's life had been no bed of roses. He had been in all the worst corners of all the continents of the world, looking for freaks and animals; and his childhood had been spent with the Wild West Show in which his mother was a rider. His father had been a carnival advance agent.

There were few things that could shake him, but this was one of them. For this girl was so obviously from a class of society that did not go around shooting people. She belonged among her own kind, at Miami or Newport, Park Avenue or Grosse Point, and not squatting in an abandoned hotel between the deserted beach and a swamp.

Dave lit a cigarette and tucked it between his lips while he opened the larger of his grips. He extracted an Army .45 automatic, wiped the excess grease off it, and shoved a clip into the butt. On second thought, he worked a cartridge into the chamber; might as well be ready for anything. The leather armpit holster showed under his vestless coat, but that was just as well; maybe if these crackers up the beach knew he was armed they'd meet him with a little respect.

Rawley, he thought, standing up and throwing the cigarette away. Virginia Rawley, of Rawley Acres. A daughter, probably, of the Rawley who had killed himself when the real estate development failed. And her father's failure, the loss of the family money, had made her a little screwy.

But somehow that theory didn't hold water....

He went around a dune and came in sight of the cluster of shacks.

There were five of them, and they were not prepossessing. He selected the largest, the one from which smoke was coming, and went up. A side door, gritted with blown sand till the paint was all gone, a window with wadded newspaper replacing most of the panes, and an outside shower to wash off salt water.

DAVE MCNALLY RAPPED on the door. Then he stepped back a pace, his hands ready to go up to his armpit if necessary.

When no one answered, he rapped again.

Finally the door opened and a man stepped out. He was dressed in overalls and battered sneakers; about six feet tall, very wiry, and wasted away to a scorbutic hundred and fifty pounds. Deep hollows separated his unshaven jaws from his lackluster eyes.

To this unpromising figure there was added a rifle, cradled in the overalled arms.

"My name's McNally," Dave said pleasantly. "I'm hunting snakes for a circus. Could you put me up for a couple of nights and give me a hand in rounding up some men to go into the swamps?"

The man drawled a syllable in the flat, nasal cracker accent. The syllable was, "Naw." He started to close the door again.

"I'm not selling anything," Dave said. He tried a disarming grin; the cracker remained armed. "I can pay two dollars a night for my room and board, and I'll pay five dollars a day each for three men to help me round up these snakes."

The cracker said, "Naw." But there was a little interest in his eyes.

"That's thirty-four dollars for two days," Dave said, encouraged. "The man who helped me could have it all, and pay his two helpers whatever they had to have out of it."

Automatically the cracker's lips got round, with another *N*—but then he stepped out and closed the door behind him. "Could bring a pa'r of snakes into town foah you," he said. "Ten dollars each."

This was getting some place. "Go on," Dave said gently, "any cracker in Florida will go into the swamps and bring me a pair of cottonmouths and a 'gator for a five dollar bill. I want *big* snakes. Half a foot through, and ten feet long."

"They's in the swamps, misteh. I could git 'em foh yuh. Biggest snakes in Floridy."

"Those are the ones," Dave said. "Only my time's worth money. I want to go along, and get this over with. I don't want to have to stay here more than two days."

The cracker was definitely interested now. "Ah kin git 'em, misteh. Yuh ask innybody in St. Michael. Lafe Overholt's bin around these swamps all his life, they'll tell yuh, 'n' he ain't scared of nothin'."

Some devil in Dave made him ask, "Nothing?"

Lafe Overholt's face hardened… like the taxi driver's

had done. He said, "Naw," and reached behind him for the doorknob. The paintless door slammed in Dave's face.

As Dave turned around he saw faces disappearing through the dirty windows of the other shacks. He knocked on each of the three doors in turn; when there was no answer, he yelled, "Well, I'll be camping on the beach. Come talk it over if you want that money."

THERE WAS A path from the shacks to the beach. He carried his bags down it, dumped them above the high-water line, and dragged down a piece of driftwood stump to sit on. There was some bar chocolate, emergency rations, in his suitcase; he got out a bar and chewed on it. The surf looked attractive, and he was hot; but he certainly couldn't afford to leave his automatic on the beach.

He took a chance on the bags, though, and when he had finished the chocolate walked back toward Overholt's place. As he came up the path, some towheaded kids squealed and ran away through the salt hay.

Dave got himself a drink from the outside shower at Lafe Overholt's house, and then went back to the beach. He took a rubber poncho from his bag, stretched it on the sand, and lay down, his head pillowed on the smaller suitcase. At least, it didn't look like rain.

If a man has to sleep on a beach, there are worse places for it than Florida. The breeze off the ocean kept the insects moving; it was not too cold; and as it got dark and the stars came out, the porpoises leaping just off the shore sent arcs of luminescence through the night to entertain him.

Lying there in his shirt and trousers, Dave McNally finally rolled himself into his poncho and went to sleep.

He had been hungrier in his life, and dirtier, and had slept on more uncomfortable places.

He was awakened at eleven by a motorcar. He sat up abruptly, hand on his gun; lights were coming swiftly along the beach. The tide was out, and the car was making good time on the hard-packed sand. Dave pulled on his shoes and ran down toward the tidal beach.

Shells crunched under his feet. He got to the middle of the wide beach when the headlights were still a hundred yards away, projected himself into their gleam, and waved his arms. Brakes screamed, and for a moment he thought the car was going to be unable to stop before it hit him; but it went into a skid, and stopped about fifty feet opposite him. A flashlight played on him, nearly blinding him.

A voice called, "What do you want?"

"I'm camping up by Overholt's," Dave began.

"Yeah? That him, mister?" the voice asked someone else in the car. It was a Florida voice.

Another, more Northern accent said, "No, neither of 'em."

The first voice cried, "Stay away from this car. We don't want no trouble till we're sure." The car went into gear and away, its motor drowning out Dave's voice.

Dave McNally gently scratched his head, muttered, "Southern hospitality," and went back to his sandy bed.

But not to sleep. Coming up the path, his feet noiseless in the dry, loose sand, he made out a figure stooping over his bags. His temper snapped. "Throw up your hands and stand still!"

His own flashlight went on after he had dropped to the sand, the gun out. People shoot at flashlights. But this one didn't. It was the girl, Virginia Rawley. She didn't seem to have the rifle with her.

HE LET THE flashlight go out, then made a swift, bent-over run that brought him right up to her. If he got right on her, none of her strange friends could dare shoot without taking a chance of hitting her.

He flung an arm around her waist, pulled her to him. She struggled.

"This isn't love," he muttered. "I'm holding you as a shield, in case you've got Overholt ambushing me." Her waist was firm and muscular under his hand.

She stopped struggling, relaxed. "I'm all alone. I came out to talk to you."

"Word of honor?" He grinned in the dark at the childish phrase.

"Word of honor," she said. As he let her go, she sat down on the sand next to the poncho.

Dave McNally crouched beside her, said, "Cigarette? They can't see us here, the dunes protect us."

"All right." She accepted a cigarette and a light, puffed once, the glow setting off her fine, delicate features. She said, "There a filling station about four miles from the beach. It's on the main highway into St. Michael's. You can get up there by three o'clock; there's a milk truck comes along then that'll take you into town."

"But I'm not going to town," Dave said. "I invested in a railroad ticket to come down here and get some snakes. I'm going to get them."

"That's the most ridiculous story. You could have stopped at St. Augustine, or even Jacksonville, and sat in your hotel lobby, and the natives would have caught all the snakes you can use. Don't tell me you're a scientist, looking for a rare specimen. You are not the type."

"Not intellectual enough, eh?" Dave growled. "Well, while we're playing truths, you're not the type to bury herself in a ramshackle hotel like that little ruin you're living in. Would you, since my roofless condition seems to give you insomnia, mind explaining what this is all about? I come down here to wrestle a couple of snakes, and everybody in the county starts shooting at me. I didn't know you prized your snakes so highly in Florida."

He felt around behind him for his coat, got out his wallet. "Here's my business card. Amusements and Expeditions. I want two very long snakes for a sideshow at Coney Island. I know I could buy them, but by sending me down, the man who wants them figured he could cut the time by two weeks. Two weeks, lady, is something like ten per cent of a Coney Island season. It means the difference between a profit and going broke."

She examined the card in the glow from her cigarette. "You sound almost convincing," she murmured. "Isn't there any other place you can get these snakes? I thought the biggest ones' came from South America."

"Sure they do, pal," Dave said. He felt he was getting some place at last. "But the P.A. won't carry them on their planes, and it would take six weeks or two months to get them up on a freighter. See?" He took a deep breath. "Look," he said, "if you're in some jam with the law—you and your cracker friends—why, that's all right with me. You don't get ahead in the carnival trades by running to the sheriff every time you see someone breaking the parking law. All I want is my snakes, and a lift to the nearest railroad for the big city."

"I almost believe you. Well—pick up your bags. You might as well sleep at the hotel tonight."

HE WALKED ALONG behind her, carrying the heavy bags once more, the automatic swinging against his chest. He was a little breathless when they got to the house.

She said, "Take the room up there on the gallery. That bed has the least number of springs broken. I'll make you some supper."

He grinned at her with depthless gratitude, and lugged his bags upstairs. When he came down he was still wearing the automatic, but he had buttoned his coat over it. He put a flask of brandy on the kitchen table. "For the coffee," he said. Straddling a kitchen chair, he watched the girl moving around the big kitchen, frying eggs, opening a can of tomatoes.

When the food was ready she set out two coffee cups. "I haven't had a coffee and brandy in months," she said. For all her youth, her eyes looked a little tired.

Dave McNally forked in food, then suddenly said, "Look, it's against all the rules of my business to step into trouble when I don't have to—but can I help you in this jam you're in?"

She shook her head. "No, thanks. I—it isn't my secret to tell you, anyway."

"O.K., pal. That was the law I talked to on the beach before, wasn't it?"

"That's right. The sheriff. Going to run to him?"

"And get held here as a witness, when I ought to be in New York?"

She smiled. "Tough, aren't you? If you want to bathe, there's a bathroom next to yours. But there's only cold water."

"O.K. See you in the morning. Can you get me a guide into the swamps?"

"I'll talk it over with the Overholts," the girl said. She smiled wearily and went upstairs.

Dave McNally finished his coffee, smoked a cigarette, and then turned out the lights and went across the ballroom to the stairs that led up to his room. He had not seen his rifle. Presumably it was in Virginia Rawley's bedroom, some place in the old building.

It was too bad, he thought, about repeal. If there were still bootleggers and rum-runners, he would know what to make of this, what line to take.

3

INTO THE SWAMP

WHEN HE CAME down in the morning, there was conversation in the kitchen. He went across the ballroom, his feet making scraping noises as they drove the sand into the maple floor. Virginia Rawley was talking to Lafe Overholt and another man who was obviously some kin to Overholt, though he was shorter, narrower, and in much better health. They grinned at Dave with what was meant to seem like friendliness.

"This is Lafe Overholt," the girl said, "and his brother Mark. They're going to take you out in the swamps after your snakes today."

So that was all there was to it? These were like mountaineers, surly to all strangers, but friendly enough if you gave them a drink and time to get used to you.

Dave sat down opposite the Overholts. "Know where I can find the big ones, boys?"

"Over by Salt Run, this time yeah," Mark Overholt, volunteered. "They's th'oo layin' their aigs now, an' they go down theah for the hawgs. Couldn't sell ya a passel of wild hawgs, could we, misteh? Go right well in thet circus Miss Rawley been tellin's 'bout." Their dialect, aided by the brandy, was almost unintelligible.

The girl gave him eggs and toast and coffee. "No hogs," Dave decided. "We leave that to the customers." There was no laugh. "Have some more brandy, boys."

"Hev some yourself, misteh. Don' know as we fancy this fancy likker."

Looking at the empty bottle, Dave suppressed a grin. He ate quickly, and stood up. "I'll go upstairs and get my equipment."

" 'Quipment? All you need to ketch a snake's a pronged stick, misteh."

"Not these snakes," Dave said. "I want big ones. I've got a canvas bag to put them in when we get them. No use doing things the hard way when you don't have to."

As he went up the stairs he could hear a chuckle behind him. It was not the girl who had laughed.

"That's right," one of the Overholts said.

He got his canvas snake bag, and a short steel fishing rod that he could run a noose through. If you can hold a snake's head down, you have him. On second thought, he put another flask of brandy in his pocket; it seemed to be the solution to the Overholts. He took along a needle filled with anti-venom, and a package containing two extra clips for his automatic, and went downstairs again. He carried rubber boots in his hands.

THE OVERHOLTS SWUNG up. "S' long, Miss Rawley. Thenks foah gittin's this little job," one of them said.

The girl had not said a word since he had come down to breakfast. Just as they were leaving, though, she waved her hand and smiled. The smile was not very successful.

Well, he had nothing to fear. He was armed, and the

Overholts were not, except for a fisherman's knife at Mark Overholt's belt.

"Hope you ain't skeered of 'gators, misteh," Mark said. "They's a passel of 'em in yon."

He led the way along the trail away from the hotel. As soon as they had crossed the road down which the taxi had brought Dave the day before, the ground underfoot changed, became less sandy. In a few yards they were winding among scrub palmetto, then among true palms. The Spanish moss came down from the trees far enough to scrape the top of Lafe Overholt's hat.

They were going downhill, and moss was underfoot too. And then, abruptly, they were at the edge of the swamp. Mark Overholt cut a stalk of some weed, and began to use it for a walking stick, tapping the ground ahead of him for firmness. They went along, occasionally jumping from one hummock to another, to avoid a patch of what was apparently solid ground.

Within five minutes they were completely surrounded by trailing vines and moss and gnarled short trees. It was as though the beach and the sand were miles away. Mosquitoes descended on them in swarms, and black flies; once a spider as big as Dave's fist regarded them from its web in the branches of a live-oak.

"Theah's a snake," Lafe Overholt said. He pointed at a moccasin swimming calmly in the dark waters of the lagoon they were skirting.

"That's just a baby," Dave said.

"Sho," Mark said over his shoulder. "Jest a baby."

"Big enough to pizen yuh, though," the dour Lafe said.

Mark cried, " 'Ware 'gators!" and jumped the lagoon.

Under his feet as he went through the air were logs float-
ing—big logs with moss on their back. One of them
opened its mouth and snapped at Mark's heel with a click
like a steel trap. It was an alligator.

Lafe tried a vine, abandoned it, found another that
was strong enough to swing his ungainly body over after
his brother's. Three of the 'gators snapped this time, their
malevolent eyes blinking at the indignity of having their
rest disturbed.

When Dave jumped, he jumped so high and so hard
that the Overholts had to catch him to keep him from
going headlong into a pool of rotted vegetable matter on
the other side.

"Ef you cain't jump right," Lafe said, "better use a vine.
Cracker's railroad."

"We's neahly to Salt Run," Mark said. "Yon's egrets. Send
you to the pen foah life foah killin' one of those critters."
He pointed to a flight of white birds, startlingly beautiful.

"Game wardens in the swamps, eh?" Dave asked.

"Yeah, they visit us now an' again," Mark said. "You never
can tell."

A CRANE WHOOPED overhead, as they went on. So whatever fears Dave had had were groundless. The law patrolled
these swamps, game wardens watched every party that
came in.

At noon they came out of the swamp, or so it seemed.
Ahead of them stretched a bay of some sort, fifty, yards
across, and twisting at both ends so that its length couldn't
be estimated.

"Salt Run," Mark said. "Mought's well eat."

They sat on hummocks at the edge of the sand, and ate sandwiches that Lafe had carried.

Mark said, "Had we time, mought ketch a crab or two, and roast her."

"Gempun wants snakes," Lafe pointed out.

Mark waded Salt Run first. When Dave saw that the water scarcely reached to his knees, he pulled on the rubber boots and followed him. His feet scared up crabs and needle-fish in the clear shallow water.

On the other side, Lafe pointed. "Mought as well leave those fancy boots. Jest weigh yuh down in the swamps." His overalled legs dripped water.

Dave took off the boots, and Mark hid them under a driftwood stump.

On the other side, as soon as they had gone a hundred feet inland, the swamp closed around them again. A spring that they passed explained the vegetation; hidden springs were pouring fresh water into the swamps.

"Keep youh eyes peeled," Mark said. "See the snakes any time now."

They reached another lagoon. Mark looked up and down, then jumped. Lafe went after him, then Dave McNally got ready to jump.

Mark cried, "Snakie. Behind you, misteh."

Dave whirled. Coiled on the ground behind him was a rattler, one of the biggest he'd ever seen. But rattlers were not what he wanted. He jerked the automatic loose from its holster, and fired on the down-thrust. The rattler sprang, but it no longer had a head.

Dave put the automatic back in its holster, turned, and jumped the lagoon. He felt pretty bad; he'd collected snakes before, but he'd never gotten over his fear of them. And that had been pretty close, and plenty messy.

He said to Mark Overholt, "Not big enough. No rattler would be."

"He wants chokers," Mark said. "Follow me, misteh."

They tramped on. Dave's face felt hot and swollen from the exertion, from the damp muggy swamp air, from the mosquitoes. His head was beginning to throb from fever.

Half an hour later Mark said:

"Chokers in theah. C'mawn."

He motioned to Dave and Lafe to flank him. They went ahead in single file, putting each foot down cautiously, lest it hit quicksand.

The rays of the sinking sun were in their eyes when Mark cried:

"Choker!"

4

ABANDONED

THE TWO OVERHOLTS stepped back. Dave blinked, getting out his noosed rod. He shut his eyes to get the sun out of them, opened them again, and saw the boa, if that was what he was, lying along the ground. There was no bulge in the animal's long, thick body; it had not fed lately.

It was neither sleepy nor afraid: it was coming for him. The Overholts went back another step. The snake coiled the front half of its body and sprang.

The big snakes are not poisonous; they kill by sinking their jaws into their prey, and then winding their body around until they have choked its life out.

Dave dodged, and as the big fellow went by, swung with his rod. It was a lucky cast; the noose went over the boa's head. Dave tightened with the reel, and thrust down. The boa's head went to the marshy ground, as the hunter felt a shock run up the rod that nearly tore his shoulder loose at the socket.

He yelled: "One of you get his tail! Don't let him kink."

There was no answer, and at that moment the snake acted. His body, almost independent of his head, slashed around. Dave ducked, lying nearly flat, still holding on to the rod—but even so, the snake's scaly, cold, heavy body flicked his head. Had it hit square, he thought, it would have knocked him down, certainly knocked loose his hold on the rod, possibly stunned him.

He yelled: "Give me a hand here!" There was still no answer, and he stole a look.

His guides were gone.

It was not the first time he had known heart-chilling, breath-taking fear, but it was one of the worst times. The snake's body was writhing gently; it was getting ready for another attack against this monstrous foe who held its head down.

It was a temptation for Dave McNally to pull his gun and end it there. But snakes were what he had come to Florida for, live snakes and big ones.

He shoved the butt of the rod over a live-oak limb, pulled it down again; the snake's head went into the air. Surprised, thrown off its plan of murder by this, the charge was lost to the snake.

Before it could recover, Dave had whipped off his belt and tied the fishing rod tight against the gnarled tree trunk. The animal was left there, hanging head up, its body lashing around the trunk.

Dave dropped back, sweat covering him—cold, clammy sweat. He bawled: "Overholt! Come on back. He's tied up!"

There was no noise, no answer. The snake's wild body made thudding sounds against the tree trunk, and that was all.

HE CALLED TWICE more before he realized that this had been planned. Dave McNally, the wise guy! Lured into a Florida swamp by a couple of crackers, and left here. They had meant to do this all along. That was why they had swallowed their animosity, had become suddenly friendly. It was a trap to get rid of him.

He thought of the Rawley girl, pretty, young—and somehow she seemed more horrible, more loathsome now, than the boa striking and coiling around the trunk. She had done this to him, had sent him out into this 'gator-covered, snaky swamp, this morass of quicksands and vipers—to die.

Well, he wasn't dead yet. He started up to work on the snake. He might as well accomplish what he had come for.

Something warned him, then, to turn.

Snakes often came in pairs. This one had. The female had come from some lair, seeking its mate; and she had found Dave McNally.

As he jumped back, she sprang. She sprang low, for some reason; her mouth, fangless, closed on his boot. It was not much of a grip—but instantly the long body, nearly as thick and heavy as its mate's, kinked and then swung for the choke.

Dave's hand got his gun, Dave's arm swung it down, made the butt ring against the ophidian skull twice; he never knew he had done it.

The snake dropped away, its body unlashing, striking angrily in the other direction.

It backed off a yard, small cold eyes glittering. Dave ripped a branch off a live-oak, tearing his fingers; his strength was superhuman in his fear. He jumped before the snake could charge, and his heavy heel landed on the snake's head. He struck at her lashing body with the branch, brought his other foot down to hold her neck, released the first foot, and struck again.

The snake kinked and wound around the branch. Dave

felt a surge of triumph; he pulled the first of the canvas bags off his back, and threw it over the coil; he pushed the stick into the bag, and all of the snake except her head and neck went in. He jumped off the neck, kicked at the head, and then pulled the draw strings tight. He had his snake. In a way it had been ridiculously easy....

He made a sailor's knot in the heavy drawstrings, and took off the other sack; he had tied them to his shoulders. His hand came down bloody, and he investigated; the branch he had torn away had skinned his hand, and he had broken the string that held the sacks to his back. But he had not known it at the time, or he could not have done it; the force he had used had driven one of the strings through his shirt and into his flesh across his shoulder.

A long, straight welt was bleeding gently on his shoulder.

He sat down on the ground and was violently sick. He had never fought harder, or called on his body for more immediate, violent effort. But he had won. He had the snake.

WHEN HE COULD get up again, he took a swallow of his brandy, and tackled the male. Tired out from battling the tree, the big fellow did not give him much trouble. Just as the last rays of the sun disappeared, he bagged his second snake. He was ready to go back to New York now. Only he didn't know the way.

He sat down, lit a cigarette, tried to make a plan. The intelligent man makes a plan, he does not go barging off into the night looking for action. The intelligent man knows that he will be all right, that quicksands can be avoided with a stick, snakes and alligators fought back with an automatic. The intelligent man takes his fears and analyzes them, until they cease to be fears.

Of course he does. That quick thudding of Dave McNally's heart was just caused by overexertion in going through the swamps, in fighting with the boas. The sweat that pricked the roots of his hair and the back of his neck was from the heat.

He was not afraid. That shape over there was only a tree. He was not afraid of spending a night in the swamps. Not at all. His throat was dry because he needed water.

Water, that was it. He could not stay there because he had no drinking water. That was the reason he had to get out. The intelligent man would not drink swamp water and get some horrible disease just to avoid walking through a swamp at night.

Filled with relief because he had a sensible reason for doing the thing all his instincts called on him to do, he rose, blowing a last puff of cigarette smoke at the mosquitoes that were coming on with renewed vigor, now that it was dark. He tied the snakebags to a tree-limb; they were too heavy to carry.

The sun had gone down that way. Therefore the ocean would be in the other direction. If he could find the beach, he could follow it back to the hotel. He would be all right there, though the girl had sent him to his death. He had his gun, and she would not be expecting him back.

He unclasped his big pocket knife, and started out with a cypress limb for a walking stick. He went along very slowly, and every few yards he slashed a blaze on a tree, so as to make a trail he could find back to his snakes.

IT WAS SLOW, tough going. Tough thorns and branch tips

caught at his clothing. The mosquitoes and gnats swarmed over his face, nearly blinding him. Several times in the first few minutes his stick came down on nothing, water splashing, mud quaking, and he drew it back, thrust it around till it came to firm footing.

After ten minutes he seemed exhausted. He stopped, panting, wiping his eyes on the sleeve of his shirt.

He took a tiny swallow of brandy, rested a few minutes, went on. Almost instantly something brushed his face, and he leapt back in horror. Leapt back, one foot going onto a firm hummock, the other splashing into water....

With the aid of his stick he righted himself. He thrust the stick out in front of him; it encountered something.

Finally he struck a match. Then he grinned, wryly, ruefully. The thing that had struck his face was no snake. It was Spanish moss, hanging from a tree limb.

But as the match burnt his fingers and he had to shake it out, he saw something else. He had come to a lagoon, and a wide one.

And he had learned something else. There were very few matches in his box.

He went ahead to the edge of the lagoon. He could jump; but how did he know he would land on solid ground? He could wade, but there might be 'gators—or worse, water moccasins, in the lagoon.

Dave McNally, tough guy, stood on the edge of that little stretch of water and was afraid.

Finally he stirred the water with his stick. No 'gators thrashed, no snakes lashed at the stick. Maybe it would be all right. He lowered himself from the bank, cautiously. All right. It was hardly to his knees. He took a step forward, then another.

His foot sank on and on. He tried to pull it back. The other foot went into the mire, too, and he was caught. The soft mud pulled him down.

Dave strangled a cry in his throat and flung himself forward. His fingers caught a feel of muddy bank; nothing to catch on there. Desperately, knowing that if he failed he was dead, he lurched forward. One hand closed on a cypress root.

Inch by inch he pulled himself from the mud. Inch by painful, throat-clogging inch.... It seemed an hour till he lay on the hummocky bank, gasping.

After a while he stood up, made a blaze on a tree to show where he had crossed, and went on.

Fifteen minutes later his hand brushed a tree, then went back to brush it again.

It was one of his own blazes. Since leaving the lagoon he had, in his exhaustion, traced a circle, like any tenderfoot. He, Dave McNally, who had been to Africa after tigers, to Brazil for monkeys, up the Rima on a silly expedition for white Indians, had behaved like a tenderfoot.

Someone had said, once: "The life of an explorer's safe enough. Ten to one you won't get killed. But when you've made twenty expeditions, the odds are two to one against you."

Sitting on a hummock, he started to count how many expeditions he had been on.

"This is crazy," he muttered. "Stop it, Dave, cut it out." He didn't even know he was talking out loud, didn't know anything.

Like many a man before him, he started reciting the multiplication table. At six times seven is forty-two, he suddenly grinned. And then he knew he was going to be all right. He might fall into a hole or be bitten by a snake, but he was through being scared.

He stood up, tried to get his bearings—and the moon came out.

Dave McNally punched his mosquito-swollen jaw, and said: "O.K., pal. Let's go shoot us a couple of Overholts." Because, sleeping on the beach the night before, he had seen the moon rise in the east, over the ocean, and all his directions were O.K. now.

Twenty minutes later he smelled salt air. An hour later he was floundering down Salt Run, half swimming, half walking, his automatic ludicrously strapped to the top of his head.

Salt Run ran, as it had to do, into the ocean. He climbed out at last on the beach.

5

TWO SNAKES

BEACHES ARE ABOUT the nicest things in the world. There is no greater pleasure in the world than walking along a beach at night, though your face is puffed to twice its natural size by mosquitoes, though one hand and one shoulder is scraped and cut, though most of your clothes have been torn off, and an oyster shell has sliced through your boot sole and slashed your foot.

The very feel of the sand working into the cut is a pleasure. Because on a beach, in the moonlight, there is a hundred feet of smooth, shining sand, and nothing can sneak up on you at all.

As he had seen the natives do in the West Indies, Dave McNally changed his course a little, and walked into the ocean, until it bathed him up to the waist. Then he held his gun high and ducked under.

He couldn't be any wetter, and the good ocean washed away the mud and cleaned out, stinging cleanly, his cuts and bites. He walked on up-grade again, and continued along the beach.

Eventually the hotel bulked darkly in the moonlight. He sat down, took a sip of brandy, inspected his gun. It seemed to be in good working condition, as nearly as he could tell without actually firing it.

His feet made no noise on the soft sand as he went up the hill towards the hotel. There was a light burning in the kitchen; he crept up and peered into the dirty, sand-scratched glass.

The two Overholts, and a third man who might well have been an Overholt, were talking to a man and woman of middle age, and from their clothes, something better than middle position.

Dave McNally could not hear what they were saying. He moved down to the next window; there was a missing pane, and he could hear.

The middle-aged man said: "I'd go away, if I could, if I had any place to go. Then they could search the swamp, and find this fellow with his neck broken. Who would there be to say how it happened?"

"Nobody," Mark Overholt said. "Anyway, they wouldn't have to find him. They's quicksands 'n' muckholes in yon, no one's never plumbed." He grinned, slyly. "'At's why I raikoned 'twould be better t' leave that second Yankee alive. He'll find him a muckhole all by hisself."

"You're sure he won't get out, Mark?" the middle-aged man said.

"No, sir. No Yank could find his way out of that yere swamp. No, sir, Mr. Rawley."

MR. RAWLEY! RAWLEY, the promoter whose schemes had gone broke! The man who was supposed to have jumped off a boat! There had been someone—the taxi man—mentioned a hundred thousand dollar insurance policy. So that was what this was all about. Rawley had faked a suicide, his wife had collected the insurance, and now they lived somewhere around here, hidden by the swamps, with the Overholts to keep strangers away.

"But I haven't got any place to go," Rawley said. "I can't take a chance of being recognized. My picture was on thousands, hundreds of thousands, of folders that we sent out when we were promoting the Acres; too many people—"

Mark Overholt finished it for him: "Too many people would be pleased to see yuh in jail, misteh. I know."

Rawley flushed, and said nothing.

"Anyway," his wife said, "we couldn't do that. We can't kill Virginia, and she'd talk. She wants to leave, she hates us for leaving that second man in the swamp." The woman fluttered her hands. "But there was nothing else to do."

So the girl hadn't been in on the plot to kill him! Dave was glad, somehow.

"The snake hunter?" Mark asked.

Lafe laughed.

Dave backed away. Somebody had come in here, looking for Rawley. There must be rumors that he was still alive. The way the cab driver had frozen up, he must have believed Dave was a friend of the absconder's.

But that wasn't important. They had the girl some place, and the girl had tried to save his life. He couldn't do less for her, and anyway he wanted to find his Mannlicher. In all probability the automatic would jam when he tried to use it. Maybe she was at the Overholts....

No, of course not. They would keep her in her room, upstairs. It was logical, the thing to do.

He crept around to the far end of the hotel. The sand had drifted-high here; it covered all the downstairs windows.

But the girl would be upstairs, and she would be at this end. At least, she had put him at the other end of the gallery, and he had not heard her.

He started up the sloping pile of sand. It shifted and spilled under his feet; he went back to the bottom almost immediately. Five minutes of struggle filled his shoes and clothing with sand, and his mind with the acceptance of failure.

That left going through the kitchen, or over the rotted front porch. The Overholts would be sure to be armed now; that meant the porch.

He got around on the front. The gone-wild trees and shrubs cast shadows, made it hard for him to see what he was doing; he stumbled over a gutted cash register, and stretched full length on the ground, swearing softly.

WHEN HE FINALLY got to the porch, he bumped into it before he saw it. He stopped instantly. It seemed to him that he had made no more noise than a pair of elephants.

He inched up on the porch, lying flat on his belly, thinning his body out to cover as much area as possible, trying to keep from putting enough strain on any one point to go through.

He made the wall of the hotel that way. To his other troubles were now added a few splinters. His hands explored the wall above his head, feeling for a window. He found one, but it was, miraculously, intact. He crept upon the porch. Here was one that was broken, but the jagged edges of glass were still stuck in the woodwork.

He knelt, praying every moment that he would not go through the porch, and worked on the glass with his swollen hands, laying each piece beside him as he got it out.

One chunk stuck, and he had to take the putty out bit by bit with his knife.

All the time he could hear the steady hum of conversation in the kitchen.

The last piece of glass came out. He put his hands on the sill, slowly hoisted his body up, letting his feet trail. He was half through now, more; there was the problem of landing inside without noise.

He managed it by letting himself slump through, landing on his shoulder with only a dull thud, then pulling his legs down on top of him.

The stairs ought to be that way, through the dark. Dave went along slowly, pushing one ragged boot and then the other, fearful that he would upset a chair in the dark....

His hand closed on the newel post. He went around it, and was on the stairs. He climbed one step, two—

The lights went on, and Mark Overholt yelled something unintelligible.

Dave made a wild scramble up the stairs.

A rifle crashed, and a bullet smacked into the splintering wood with a wicked, singing noise.

He turned, the automatic ready, the safety unthumbed. He saw Mark in the kitchen doorway, the lean Lafe behind him, the rest of them crowding through. He squeezed the .45.

And as he feared, it jammed. The automatic is no gun to fill with sand and mud.

MARK'S RIFLE CAME up again, pointing at him. Mark's face cuddled against the stock.

Dave heaved the automatic straight at the cracker. Mark fired, the rifle bullet doing something to the ceiling of the ballroom. A bloody smear became one side of Overholt's face, and he tumbled back against Lafe.

Dave McNally took the rest of the stairs in antelope leaps, yelling, "Virginia! Miss Rawley!" as he galloped along the balcony.

A man's voice bawled something from a room he had just passed.

Dave turned and flung himself against the door. It flung him tack against the creaking railing. From below two rifles thundered at the same time, and dust came down on his sweating face.

He had gathered himself for another plunge at the door when he saw that it was locked, and the key left in the hole. He stopped himself in mid-air, dropped to his knees to make as poor a target as possible, and twisted the key. He plunged into the room, yelling: "Where's that rifle? That Mannlicher?"

There was no answer. He groped for the light switch, pressed it.

Virginia Rawley was huddled in a chair, her hands tied behind her. A man was in another chair, tied hand and foot. Gagged, but the gag had slipped enough for him to have been the one who yelled at Dave.

Dave's knife tore at the cords, ripped the bandages that held the gags. "My rifle!" he said. "Damn it, where is that elephant gun?"

The girl said, foolishly, "It's the snake hunter."

"Yeah! Yeah!" Dave snapped. "Where's my gun?" Outside noises told him that the Overholts were coming up the creaking stairs.

"They've got it," the girl gasped. "And another from your suitcase."

He should have known. More to give himself time than anything else, Dave grabbed up a water pitcher and stepped onto the gallery.

Mark Overholt was half up the stairs; Rafe was still in the kitchen door.

Dave heaved the half full pitcher at Mark, and Lafe fired. The man who had been tied said, "Damn it," and sat down behind Dave.

THE HEAVY JUG landed square. Mark Overholt's bloody face snapped back, the pitcher bounced off, went over the railing, smashed.

Mark let go of the gun, and as he jackknifed backwards, the rifle bounced into the air, landed on the steps higher than Mark had been.

Dave jumped the railing, got down the steps, got the gun before Mark could recover. It was a .22 repeater, which explained why there had not been any more casualties.

Dave flung himself down on the floor of the gallery, poked the rifle between the rails, and took careful aim at Lafe Overholt.

Lafe, in the doorway, was using his rifle like a machine gun, spraying bullets along the gallery. It seemed to be some vermin size, too. But with a .22 it is accuracy that counts.

Dave shot slowly and easily, praying each time that he had another cartridge. On the third shot, a little round hole appeared in Lafe Overholt's head, and he went over backwards. Neither the third man nor the Rawleys had appeared.

Mark Overholt, bloody and battered, went wild then. He charged up the stairs, firing Lafe's rifle as he came; it was hell on the woodwork.

Dave picked him off at the top of the stairs.

THERE WAS NO more disturbance. Dave went back to the room. The girl was mopping at the wounded man's bare chest. Dave pushed her aside, and bent over. Blood was oozing from a tiny hole.

"I think it missed the lungs," Dave said. "You can't be sure, though."

The girl said, "We'll have to get him to a doctor."

"So you use doctors down here?" Dave asked bitterly. "I thought maybe you just said a chant at the dark of the moon. In case you're interested, I just killed Mark and Lafe Overholt. You might say thank you; they were sitting in the kitchen getting ready to knock you off when I got there. I don't know what happened to the other man that was there, or to your father and mother."

"They aren't my father and mother," the girl said. "My uncle and his wife. I—I didn't know my uncle was even alive. My aunt got me down here. She wanted me to sell some stocks and things. She—"

"All right, all right. Who's the boy friend here?"

"A detective from the insurance company. Weren't you looking for him?"

"No, pal," Dave said wearily. "I was looking for snakes. But nuts with that. I have to find that other cracker, also your uncle."

"I think my uncle and aunt went away," Virginia Rawley said. "And Jase Overholt has a broken shoulder. He was trying to fire off your big rifle."

Dave sat down. "O.K.," he said. "Don't talk. Let me rest...."

But the girl talked on.

When she had gotten to Rawley Acres she had been somewhat alarmed. There didn't seem to be any reason why a woman like her aunt—wealthy, fond of luxury—should want to stay at a battered place like this.

Then it developed that there were some bonds cached here that should have gone to the receivers when the Acres promotion went broke. She wanted Virginia to cash them for her. The girl refused.

At this point Uncle George himself came out of the swamps, and argued with her.

But while he was doing it, the insurance detective arrived. They had captured him, tied him up. Mrs. Rawley had been against killing him. And yet....

They had persuaded the girl, when Dave got there, to stall him off. They were sure he was looking for the captured insurance man.

She had said the easiest way to get rid of him was to take him to the swamps, and capture the snakes for him. Then he would have no further excuse to stay on. Her uncle's henchmen, the Overholts, had agreed—too readily.

Then, at noon that day, Jase Overholt had started going through Dave's bags. He had taken down his Mannlicher too, announced that he was going to try it out against a sand dune target.

The girl had protested that Dave would be mad if they fooled with his things, and Jase had laughed. It was then that she knew, for the first time, that they meant to leave Dave in the swamps.

She had threatened to go down for the sheriff, and they had tied her. She had heard the Mannlicher go off, and Jase screaming that it had broken his arm. They had untied her long enough to help set the arm, then tied her again and put her with the insurance dick.

She was sure they had meant to kill her.

DAVE HEARD THE story with lackluster eyes. He had done his best. He had done more than any two guys could be expected to, and now he had to make the six mile trek to—

A voice in the door said: "Put 'em up, all of you. There's a car comin' an' you have to—"

It was Jase Overholt. His one arm was still in a sling; but he was holding Lafe's .22 with the other, pressing it tight against his good shoulder, his finger against the trigger.

"Keep 'em up," he droned.

The girl, nervously, quickly screamed. Jase swiveled towards her, the gun following—and Dave dived.

As he hit the cracker around the waist, his arms tightening on the lean body, he felt the .22 barrel come down on his back. He heard the report in his ear, one of his legs went limp.

He let go, slid his locked arms higher, threw himself forward again. Jase Overholt went down backwards, his forehead striking Dave's teeth.

He kicked, hard, with his knee, trying to get the cracker's groin. He missed. He let go with his arms and groped for Jase's throat, fighting to the death, knowing this was the end.

Something crashed on his head, and then there was blackness.

A VOICE SAID: "Mike, you ought to be shot. You just

walked up and told them you were looking for this Rawley for the insurance company?"

"I was shot," another voice said. "You say I'll be all right?"

"All right, but unemployed."

A Florida voice said: "The circus man's comin' to. Hey, take it easy, lady."

Soft arms went around Dave's battered neck, a soft voice said: "I'm sorry. I'm so sorry. I meant to knock Jase out with the rifle barrel, and I got both of you. I—I might have killed you. I'm so sorry."

What was left of Dave that could feel knew that the girl felt pretty good. But he disentangled himself and sat up. His head ached horribly.

One of the three men in the room wore a star. Dave said: "If this is all over, Sheriff, I have a couple of snakes in the swamps. Can you get me two men, early in the morning, to carry them out?"

The sheriff blinked and drawled, "I reckon. Yeah, it's all over, suh, thanks to you. We caught the Rawleys comin' down the beach."

"No thanks to me," Dave said crisply. "This insurance man did it all. I just happened in at the end. You hear? I can't stay here and attend any trials. I want to be on the train for New York tomorrow."

"All right, suh," the sheriff said. "Feelin' around here is that anything that you want is yours. We sure don't like that George Rawley.... But I reckon you won't be bound North alone." He looked coyly at Virginia.

Dave felt the top of his head gingerly. Then he smiled. "No, not alone," he muttered. "I'll have two snakes with me." He did not look at the girl.

GORILLA CARGO

*One gorilla makes a cargo—when that ape
is Thurston, the monkey trained in magic!*

1

THE MESSAGE

THE HOTEL DE l'Univers et de le Guerre de 1914—no fooling—boasted a tiled public room somewhat reminiscent of an unwashed dairy lunch room. It was open at the front to the street of the town of Joffre, Ivory Coast, French West Africa, and the honored guest—in this case, Dave McNally—could sit there and watch the passing throng.

Said throng was completely black. There were, besides Dave, two white men in town, the representatives of the French Government. One of these, the military man, was up and about; the other, Dr. Malgrin, had gone to bed with malaria.

Dave tinkered miserably with a small ice-making machine that the proprietor of the hotel had asked him to fix. It was an old one, a little hand machine consisting of balls and valves and a crank that, if turned hard enough, would turn a few teaspoonfuls of water into a lump of ice the size of a walnut. It no longer worked.

A big dark-skinned Portuguese, clad in the tattered remnants of a pair of blue denim pants and the more tattered remains of a Panama hat, detached himself from the crowd in the street and came through the archway into the public room.

*Thurston grabbed
at Dave and
pulled him close*

Instantly the mulatto proprietor awoke from a sleep on the desk, and cursed the breed. The Hotel de l'Univers, etc., said the proprietor, was for gentlemen who wore shirts, and not for shoeless sons of the jungle apes.

Dave McNally did not look up.

The Portuguese groped inside the Panama and produced the cleft stick that takes the place of a Western Union or Post Office cap in Africa. There was a message pinned in the cleft. *"Pour le M'sieur* Mister Seenyor Magnation," he explained.

Dave still didn't look up. *"De le Chef* Zooambe?" he asked. *"Non, Monsieur."*

"I don't want to see it, then," Dave said. "Get out." He spoke in English.

The Portuguese 'breed thrust the piece of paper under Dave's nose. McNally half raised his eyes, and put up a tired hand to swat the cleft stick, as though it were a fly. He had been sitting very quietly, because so much as lighting a cigarette started him sweating again. An American thermometer would have read 110, and it was so damp that water dripped off the ceiling.

Before he had touched the message, his eye caught it, and he said, *"Attendez."* He took the card, staring at it in disbelief.

It was a membership card in the S.A.M., the Society of American Magicians. It was out of date by five years, but it was still in good repair. It had been endorsed to one Samuel Nichols (The Great Zeroni). At least, that was what the card said.

In French, Dave said to the proprietor, "Ask him where he got this."

The mulatto spoke lingua franca at the messenger for a while. The Portuguese answered him in the same mixture of French, Portuguese, Dutch, Coptic, English and some more tongues that passed for language on the Ivory Coast. Finally the proprietor said, "He says ten miles inland. In the jungle, away from the river. He says it belongs to his employer. He is dying, this employer. I do not believe him."

Dave shrugged. "Tell him to tell his employer to come on in to see me, and I'll buy him a drink in the name of Houdini."

"He says his employer is dying. Of the bloody flux."

"Amoebic dysentery, huh?" The American showman frowned. His negotiations with the Chief Zooambe, regarding the chief and his tribe appearing in a Centennial as an African village, would take another week. "All right. Put this boy up in the shed behind the hotel, give him something to eat, and tell him I'll start with him right after cock crow."

The proprietor explained this to the messenger, speaking nicely now, because the Portuguese was going to be the cause of more money in the hotel's till. The messenger shook his head. He made an attempt to speak French.

"Pas du temps, 'sieur." His hands shook descriptively.

"Not enough time, huh?" McNally stood up, brushing

the ice machine to one side. He looked at the descriptively shaking hands of the black. "Got the shakes, has he? I'll go tonight."

"But, *M'sieur*," the proprietor objected. "That is not safe. Not at night, through the jungle, with a messenger you do not know. Perhaps you—"

The bush man had been looking from one to the other of them. Suddenly he broke into a perfect flood of language. The proprietor questioned him, then translated. "He says his *chef* says to tell you if you would not come, that he has an attraction for you that would—I do not understand this—go at a gallop for eighteen weeks at the Palace of Monsieur Keith."

"Huh?" The lethargy of staying too long on the steamy West Coast fell away for a moment. "A show that would run eighteen weeks at Keith's Palace, eh?" Dave grinned. "The guy's authentic Broadway, anyway. O.K. Tell this man to eat while I go up to my room and get my stuff together."

AS SOON AS they left the town, they were in the jungle. The guide went first, carrying a torch in one hand, a machete in the other to hack at the trailing vines and brush that blocked the path from time to time. On his back was Dave's knapsack, marked plainly, "Dave McNally, Expeditions & Amusements, Times Square, N.Y., U.S.A."

McNally carried a rifle, and he had a .45 and a canteen strapped to his waist. The .45 was a revolver; an automatic fired more shots, loaded easier, and was nicer to carry, but his had jammed on him once in Florida when he needed it most, and he carried it no longer.

Their passage awakened all the folk of the jungle. A band of small monkeys swung, chattering overhead; not far enough away, a lion roared. At his roar, two hyenas stopped laughing abruptly; but a troop of parrots woke up and began screaming insolently.

Dave tried to think of the French for snakes, to ask the carrier if they were likely to run into any; but the words escaped him.

It was hot, hotter than the subway at rush hour in July. Dave had put on a short-sleeve khaki shirt and khaki shorts for the trip; he wore the white pith sun helmet that is standard in West Africa, to the annoyance of the French, who think it looks English. Sweat streamed down his face, soaked his shirt, ran down his bare knees.

The guide went on ahead, obviously cutting down his pace to the American's. The hotel proprietor had been right; it was a lovely place to murder a man. The guns that Dave carried would provide a king's wealth to any jungle native.

The rifle was loaded, and a split second would send a bullet crashing into the guide's back; but that would do no good, for if this was an ambush, there would be other men to drop down from trees, to land unexpectedly on the shoulders under the white helmet.

But there was not much fear in Dave McNally—not just now. That S.A.M. card had seemed authentic, it had added a touch to the expedition that would be too bizarre for a common African bushwhacking.

On the other hand, he did not have much hope that the tremendous "Attraction" would turn out to be anything. Probably the Great Zeroni, Samuel Nichols, had worked out a new way of vanishing a rabbit; magicians were all screwy, and five years in the jungle would not make one saner.

McNally slugged along behind the black. This was not dancing on the Hotel Astor Roof, but then it was not handling a side show of freaks for a carnival company, either. It rated just about between those two for enjoyment.

It was just dawn when they reached the clearing.

The runner slipped out of the knapsack straps and hung the bag on a pole. Then he dropped to the ground and went to sleep, unconcernedly, his work done. A very fat black woman in a black dress came out of a hut, and said, "Mister McNally?"

"Yeah. You speak English?"

"Non." She put her head on her folded hands and tilted it to one side.

"He's asleep, eh? I'll wait. What are you, his secretary?"

The woman stared at him, not understanding. Dave grinned, and she grinned back. He went to the knapsack, got out a bottle of Three Star Brandy and a bottle of native palm wine. He handed the latter to the fat woman, and went to sit near a little fire smoldering in the middle of the clearing. Uncorking the bottle, he alternated tiny sips of the brandy with puffs on a cigarette. This was West Africa's one half hour of coolness a day, and he intended to make the most of it.

AFTER A WHILE, the woman came and motioned to him to follow her. He carried the brandy with him. It was dark inside the hut, and he didn't see the man at first.

"So you come, McNally. Good boy. I—did you bring my card back?" The voice was very weak. The man, now he could see on the pile of straw, could have almost gotten work at Ringling's as the walking skeleton.

McNally fumbled in his pockets for the S.A.M. card, handed it down. "So you're the Great Zeroni?" he asked. "How did you get 'way out here?"

"You've heard of me?" the dying man asked eagerly.

"Sure," Dave lied. "You used to play the Loew Time."

"Loew Time, Pan Time, Sun Time," the magician named the vaudeville circuits. "I was good for thirteen weeks on the Keith Time, too, any time I wanted it.... I came out here with a trading expedition. This man told me the natives were crazy about magic, they'd do anything, give anything for a new piece of voodoo."

"And it didn't work, eh?" Dave's voice was kind. "Here, take some brandy. I brought it for you. Doctors prescribe it for amoebic."

The magician shook his head.

"It's too late for any kind of medicine, McNally, but thanks. I—I don't make such a flash appearance any more. My ribs are almost sticking through my skin." He cleared his throat. "No, our expedition didn't work. Too many people had done it before.... But they like my act, McNally. The natives have been good to me."

"Well, you'll have to go back now. I'm taking you to a hospital in a little while."

"I'd never live to get there," the Great Zeroni said. "I know—I can make your fortune."

Dave said, "Yeah?"

"I've got the finest attraction.... Play Keith Time, go with the circus in the summer.... Grief, you could hire the Hippodrome, and fill it every night."

"O.K., O.K. There's plenty of time, take it easy."

"No time at all… won't last to sundown. Take you to see it. But first—if you like it—give my wife some money, huh?"

"Your wife?"

"The woman who brought you in here."

"Oh," a lot of things were coming clear to Dave McNally. "Sure, I'll look after—"

"Ten dollars American would keep her the rest of her life. Come on, help me up. I've got him down—"

"Him? Say, what is this, anyway? Animal, or freak?"

"I—don't know." Sam Nichols stopped getting up, and sat on his straw bed. "You tell me. It's the biggest—damned—gorilla you ever saw, and so smart I've trained him to do—a little magic and—fire a gun."

McNally swallowed, and said, "O.K. We'll see him later. You better rest now."

"No, now. Got to tell him—to go with you. He—come see him."

Dave humored the fevered man, and helped him up, put an arm around him to aid Nichols in walking. He didn't expect to see the phenomenon that the magician had described, but it was noticeable that none of the solicitous blacks would go with them any farther than the edge of the clearing. There was something up the path that they didn't care to visit.

2

THE GREATEST ACT

NO BREAKFAST, NO sleep, and piloting a vaudeville magician down a West African path in the early dawn light. Well, Dave McNally's business was crazy enough, but this topped it all.

They went around a big, mahogany tree, and there he was. He had a handcuff around one wrist, fastened by a chain to the base of the mahogany. "My old escape cuffs that I used in the act," Sam Nichols explained.

McNally stopped so suddenly that he let the magician slump to the ground. That gorilla must have weighed three hundred pounds; he was fully six feet tall, and that much around the chest. His hair was a deep brown, and it covered him all over; only his face and hands and feet were bare. The skin on that face was a deep chocolate brown, too, and wrinkled. It was like the face of an elderly, kindly man; till you saw the eyes. Behind their liquid brownness there was a red glow that—

The ape was whining gently, weaving back and forward. Suddenly he lurched forward, moving with his knuckles against the ground, using his arms as crutches to speed his bow legs along.

McNally's hand went to the .45 at his belt.

But Sam Nichols said, "No!" in his clipped, Broadway way of speaking. The gorilla was by him then, and Dave half shut his eyes, knowing that horrible death was next. Then his stomach was a ball of ice that threatened to rise and choke him.

The gorilla—ah, the gorilla—gathered Sam Nichols up in his arms as gently as a baby, cuddled him there, ran those brown hands over the actor's face, smoothing it, babying it.

It was the weirdest sight that ever an African sun had seen.

"O.K., big fella," Sam said feebly. "O.K., Thurston. Take me over to McNally here. Take me to McNally. He's a booking agent, Thurston, see, gonna get you on the big time, playin' forty weeks a year. Like I told you, Thurston. They'll hold you over so long at the Palace you'll have squatters' rights. Come on, trouper; this guy's come all the way from Times Square to catch your act."

And the gorilla did what he was told! He carried Sam Nichols over to Dave and set the magician down. He held out his hand.

It took as much courage as Dave McNally had ever needed in his life, but he did it. He shook hands with Thurston, the gorilla. Shook hands without putting the other hand on his gun. And the big ape pressed that hand as gently as a woman.

"Does he—does he talk?" Dave asked.

"Everything but," Sam Nichols said. "He's only a baby, nine years old. Maybe that'll come later."

"Yeah, maybe," Dave said. "Sure. I—how about his act?"

Sam Nichols lowered himself till he sat against the mahogany tree. "O.K., Thurston," he said. He stopped to look up at Dave. "Maybe we better change his name. Maybe one Thurston on the big time is enough."

"Howard Thurston's dead," Dave said. "Been dead a year."

"Oh, yeah? O.K., then." Nichols pulled a mouth organ out of his pocket, said, "Overture," and began playing "The Turkish Patrol."

The ape rattled his handcuff and stood there.

"Sure," Nichols said. He fished a key out of his pocket, unlocked the monstrous beast, and began playing again.

Thurston ambled to the middle of the clearing, faced them, bowed. Then he went into his hut, came back with a box. He set it down, opened it, took two Indian clubs. Nichols switched from the tune to "Dardanella." The ape began juggling with the Indian clubs; suddenly one of them disappeared.

Bowing, Thurston set the other down, showed his empty hands, picked up a cloth from the open top of the chest, veiled the Indian club. Also from the chest he took a small revolver; Dave McNally couldn't keep his hand from his .45 this time.

But Thurston clumsily pointed the gun at the covered Indian club, clumsily fired it in his heavy palm. It was a blank, and Dave breathed easier again.

With his eyes still on the two-man audience, the ape put his hands on the ground on either side of the cloth, swung his bowed legs into the air, and stood on his hands over the club. He lifted the cloth with his teeth and—there were two clubs.

SAM NICHOLS, THE Great Zeroni, applauded feebly. Dave joined in, while Thurston bowed anxiously, one hand below the lowest of his great ribs.

"How—how did he do that?" Dave asked weakly.

The Great Zeroni said, contemptuously, "Blackstone clubs. One fits into the other—springs."

"Oh."

"Maybe you better get a magician to help you. Sort of a stage manager."

"Yeah, I will." The ape was doing card tricks now. It was just too much.

While Thurston was taking his bow for the card tricks, Nichols handed Dave the handcuffs. "Escape act," he said. "Put them on him."

"Those are the same cuffs you use to hold him."

"Sure: I—only trained him—to get out of them when one isn't fastened to the tree. When there isn't—a chain on the end."

"Oh." Dave McNally went forward. He kept his feet firm, his hands from shaking, but he knew enough about animals to know that they could smell fear. And he was plenty afraid. He tried thinking of Thurston as a man, with the result that he caught himself saying, "Sorry, old man," when he fitted the bracelets on and fastened them.

Thurston paid no more attention to the remark than it deserved. He held out his cuffed wrists for Dave to examine; the showman had seen enough magic acts to know what was expected of him.

He tugged at the cuffs, to show the audience they were on firmly.

Then he stepped back, and Nichols went on playing his mouth organ. Thurston tugged at the cuffs as though they enraged him. He tried to get them off with his teeth. He bellowed with rage, and then, just as McNally was going forward to help, the big ape suddenly did a somersault, and came up—with the cuffs off.

This time Dave's applause was spontaneous.

"O.K.," Nichols said. "That's the act. It's taken me five years to teach him that, and how to throw a knife, how to shoot a gun. Any time you put up a target, and hand Thurston a pistol, he'll fire at the target. Hand him a knife, and he'll throw it. See? You'll have to have a pretty girl to hand him the stuff; bill it as Beauty and the Beast. Fill in the act with—"

"Wait a minute," Dave said. "Does he ever hit the target?"

Nichols said, "Hell, no. The gun's loaded with blanks, the knives are rubber painted silver. You fake it, punk. You got to get a magician to help you; he shoves the knives in from the back of the target."

"Oh."

"Fill in the act with strong man stuff," Nichols said. "Give Thurston anything and say break it, and he'll break it. You know, crowbars, horseshoes, telephone book. You get it?"

"The greatest act—" Dave began.

"You're tellin' me? An' I won't ever see— It doesn't matter. Thurston! Put the box away, bring me the cuffs. That's a good boy." He refastened the gorilla to his chain, then reached out, and gave Dave the key. "See, kid? Thurston, here's your new boss. I gotta—go away. Give me your hand, McNally."

He put Dave's hand in the gorilla's, laid his own on top. "New boss, Thurston. Come on, McNally, take me back to the hut."

ALL MORNING, DAVE sat beside the dying man's cot.

Nichols was out of his head now; his talk was all of five years ago, in split week bookings and sleeper jumps, thirteen weeks on the small time, the talkies now, they'd never hurt the old four a day. A little after noon he snapped out of it long enough to tell McNally, "Take Thurston his lunch. About three pounds of meat. He gets bananas for breakfast, and potatoes with gravy for supper. He likes apples, too."

McNally got the meat from the fat woman whom Nichols had called his wife, and took it to the ape's clearing. Thurston was sitting under the tree, on the chest that held his magic paraphernalia. He looked up when McNally came into sight, lumbered over docilely enough to take his dinner into his hands. Then, the minute his flat nostrils caught the meat odor, he was a jungle animal again; tearing and snarling at the meat, thrusting big gobs into his mouth, gulping it down. McNally went away.

Nichols was asleep. A little before dusk he awoke. "I'm— going now," he said. "When you take—Thurston out—lead him down the beach path. I don't want him to know— about me. So long, pal, I gotta— Look, you treat that ape O.K., see?"

"Yeah, sure I will. Sure, Nichols. Take it easy, boy, we're going to the—"

"Not me. I'm checking out. I—look, McNally, would you—I mean—"

"Sure, what is it?"

"When you make some dough from Thurston—run an ad—an obituary, like—in the *Billboard* and *Variety?* Huh? About how the Great Zeroni cashed in, see, only first he left his profession, the greatest act— Yuh get it?"

"Yeah. I'll do that, Sam. Lie back now."

"Sure. I think I hear the music for—my walk on."

And he died.

3

ON THE WAY

THEY BURIED HIM in the morning. McNally made a simple wooden cross, and put the old S.A.M. card in a celluloid frame from his own wallet. He tacked that on the cross, and mumbled the only prayer he knew, one remembered from childhood. The fat woman and the big Portuguese half breed stood by, wondering.

Then Dave fished what money he had with him out of his pockets, and gave it to the woman. It came to about twenty dollars in American money, all he had besides his travelers' checks. When he walked away, the woman was still standing beside the grave, staring at the money, and the big guide was staring at her. Africa does not remember long.

He put on his knapsack, loaded his guns, and smoked a cigarette. He knew that what he ought to do was go into town, and send off a radiogram from Joffre for an iron cage and a crew of animal men to come and help him. But if he left—

Well, it was obvious that none of the blacks would feed Thurston; and after that exhibition of hunger at noon yesterday, it was pretty certain that the ape would not stay handcuffed unless he was fed regularly and often, and a lot.

And Dave had a fortune in his hands. Thurston was worth more money than all the other animals in Africa, from a showman's point of view. Five thousand a week was sucker money for exhibiting the biggest gorilla in captivity—and the only one who could do tricks.

Three hundred pounds of ape that was as docile as a sixty-pound chimp!

He ground the cigarette into the earth and went out to feed Thurston. While the gorilla was eating, he opened the magic apparatus case, and got out a piece of rope. He tied this around the chest, and took the case over to Thurston.

The gorilla peeled bananas docilely, ate them, looked around for more, and, satisfied there were no more, waited for orders. Dave handed him the chest and said, "Carry it."

He couldn't be sure that Thurston understood, but he seemed to. At any rate, he picked up the case, and stood waiting while Dave unfastened the chain from the tree, and said, "Go ahead. We're going to town."

Thurston stood still.

Dave sighed and led the way, holding the chain in one hand and his rifle in the other. There were things he would rather have done than walk through the jungle with that ape behind him.

They passed no blacks in the jungle. Once Dave heard the noise of a rubber-gathering crew, and he thought he saw a shiny face peer at him from behind a tree; but when they went around the tree there were no natives.

Possibly Thurston had something to do with that.

And when they got to Joffre, that once teeming town seemed to be deserted. One dusty brown heel going up an alley constituted Dave's only glimpse of humanity. He grinned, and sought out a native butcher shop. A leg of goat seemed a tasty tidbit for Thurston; Dave took it, and shouted, "If you want your money, butcher, come to the hotel, later!"

In front of M. Dessour's home and official residence, there was a flagstaff flying the tricolor of France. Dave fastened the chain to this, giving Thurston the run of the official lawn, and handed his actor the leg of goat. Then the American turned his back.

NOW THAT THE gorilla was chained, some of the stores became attended again. Dave cashed a travelers' check at the bank, paid for the meat, and bought a large bottle of mineral water, which he uncorked and took back to Thurston, now wistfully sucking the meatless bone of the goat's leg. The gorilla seemed to know how to drink out of bottles; he took big swallows of the water, then amused himself lying on his back and seeing how far he could spurt mouthfuls of the water into the air. A respectful group of blacks gathered around him, and Thurston seemed to like the idea of an audience.

Dave went to the hotel, and asked the proprietor if any word had been gotten of a ship. The proprietor didn't know, but said that Chief Zooambe had been looking for the American.

"Tell him he can sign at my rates, or not at all," Dave said. He no longer cared about the African village for the centennial. If he could get Thurston back to America, his fortune was made.

The clerk at the radio office said there was a Dutch boat due that afternoon.

After that Dave was busy. He signed contracts with the

now meek Zooambe, made arrangements for the tribe to be aboard the freighter that afternoon. By the time he finished that, the Dutch captain was ashore.

He spoke English. "Well, Mr. McNally, you sail with us?"

"Uh-huh. I'm shipping eighteen blacks, together with their paraphernalia. They look tough, but they're tame. Can you take us straight to South America?"

"I can transship you so that you'll be there in two weeks."

"Good. We'll be aboard by the time the tide's high. Oh, and tell your cook to stock up on fresh meat; I'm bringing a gorilla with me, and he eats three pounds a day. Also bananas, plenty of—"

The captain said, "No, sir. I saw that gorilla."

"Scared of a monkey, cap?"

"Yes, sir. Of that one."

Dave tried bribery, he tried persuasion; it was no good. The ship sailed with Zooambe and his tribe, but without Dave and Thurston.

McNally bribed the radio operator to send out a general communication to all ships that an American at Joffre was willing to pay two thousand dollars to any ship that would carry him and one tame gorilla to any port in the United States.

The next morning he raised the ante to three thousand dollars, and on the third morning the tramp ship *Lorelei* dropped anchor off Joffre, and the captain came ashore looking for the American.

4

SEAGOING APE

CAPTAIN DUJARGE WAS not prepossessing. His face was an even copper color, nicely matched by teeth only one shade of yellow lighter. There was not a wrinkle or a line on that fat brown visage. He gave Dave the once-over. "American, huh? My grandpere, he was American, too. An American slave!" he added, roaring with laughter. "Me, I'm Canadian, French Canuck, and proud of it." He glared at Dave truculently.

"O.K. with me, skipper." Dave swung a leg over the arm of his chair, and yelled to the hotel proprietor to bring a bottle of cognac. "What I want to know is: How soon can we sail, and can that ship of yours get me to some American port? Miami or New Orleans would do me fine."

"We sail as soon as you can get cage and ape aboard. First we sail west, to refuel at one of the Guiana ports; then straight north. I'll have you in the U.S.A. within a month. And by the way," the captain said, "that'll be fifteen hundred now, and fifteen hundred before you land in Florida. Right?"

"Fifteen hundred when the gorilla and I come over the rail."

The captain glared, then smiled. "Hokay. I'll go out to

the ship and get a place cleared in the forepeak for the cage, and a cabin ready for you."

Dave didn't bother to tell the captain there was no cage. They could fight that out when he got aboard the ship. Thurston had begun to get a little restless. The French flagpole had developed a crack from the time the ape had awakened in the middle of the night and shaken it for amusement.

And it might be another month before a tramp ship could be found to take them. They had to leave now.

The captain left, with Dave's promise to be aboard within an hour. McNally went down to arrange for transportation out to the ship. He found that there were two kinds of boats available, beside the government's naphtha launch. One was a small rowboat; the other the deep, sturdy lighters, manned by three oarsmen standing on the stern. These latter were used to carry copra and ivory out to freighters; they stank and they leaked, but Dave wanted them.

He had no intention of getting into a rowboat with Thurston's three hundred pounds while the gorilla experienced his first sea voyage.

Hiring a lighter was not difficult; a hundred dollars would buy one. But hiring the three men to man the sweeps was a different matter. Not for all the wealth in Africa would any of the natives put to sea with Thurston.

"I will chain him," Dave promised. "At the front end of the boat. He'll not be able to reach you."

"They say," his interpreter told him, "that the ape will be able to reach the bottom of the lighter. Supposing he pulls it to pieces, like he almost did the flagpole of M. Dessour? There are sharks in the harbor."

Dave snapped his fingers. M. Dessour! His launch could pull the lighter.

The government man was more than willing. "For, consider, *M'sieur,*" he said. "For this small favor to the citizen of a friendly nation I am rid of that accursed Thurston! For three nights I have slept *chez* Dr. Malgrin, for fear that M. Thurston would find the night chilly and, breaking his chain, come to bed with me. Not even a Frenchman, *M'sieur,* could go through such an experience unshaken."

Dave laughed, and said, no, he supposed not. "I'll man the one oar myself," he said. "To steer by."

"*M'sieur,* if you will, the name of your nearest relation. For the emergency."

"There'll be no emergency. Thurston trusts me. Nichols told him to."

"An incredible story, *M'sieur.* Let us to the waterfront. I shall drive the launch myself; and I shall also see that the towrope is long."

"To the waterfront."

Dave had to buy the lighter and the oar; their owner did not expect to see them back again. He and Dessour supervised the fastening of the towrope; then Dave went back to the street and unchained Thurston from the flagpole.

The big ape seemed glad to be free again; he whimpered a little, and put his tremendous hand in Dave's.

"O.K.," the showman said. "We're off for the big time, Thurston."

At the familiar phrase from the showman's vocabulary, Thurston whimpered again. Dave carried the chain and the handcuff that were his ostensible badge of authority over Thurston; the ape carried his chest of stage apparatus in the hand that was not holding on to Dave.

The street of Joffre had once again cleared, as though by magic.

M. DESSOUR HAD already put off in his launch; it was out in the harbor, its motor idling, a long towrope leading back to the lighter, held against the shore by a rope.

Thurston went up to the waterfront willingly enough. His first sight of the ocean didn't seem to disconcert him. He even started to go down into the belly of the lighter, but at his first step the side of the boat gave under him a little and he leaped back, jerking Dave with him with a strength that nearly ripped out Dave's arm. The showman disengaged himself, became stem. "Go on. Thurston!"

The ape would not move.

Dave muttered, "Well, you can only die once." But it was not a pretty death, being torn to bits by a frightened gorilla. Nevertheless, his heart in his throat, his hands trembling and sweaty, Dave leaped, landed in the bottom of the lighter, leaving Thurston on the quay behind him.

"Come on, big fella, come on, Thurston!" he called enticingly. The ape stood on the dock, shaking a little, not liking to be alone and unfastened, but not daring to make the leap.

Dave thought, for that one moment, that, after all, show business had gotten along for a long time without Thurston. He, Dave McNally, had done all right without him. Let him go, let him run back to the jungle.

Maybe it was Sam Nichols' dying appeal, maybe it was the showman's pride in bringing back to America the greatest attraction ever put on a stage. But Dave went through with it. He put a Broadway twang into his voice, he barked words out of the corner of his mouth in as good an imitation of Sam Nichols' voice as he could muster.

"This way to the big top. This way to see the world's greatest show, Thurston, the Marvel of the Century. See him and believe him, folks, the gorilla that thinks like a man, the ape that walks like a cake eater. See—"

The words made no sense, but the tone did. With a final whimper, Thurston leaped, anxious to see who it was that was making those lively noises that he associated with his childhood, with Sam Nichols whom he had loved.

Dave dodged just in time to keep the gorilla from landing on him. The shock of the big brute's landing shook the lighter, made it rock back and forth, sent waves splashing out into the harbor. Thurston cowered in the bottom of the boat, frightened into being quiet for a moment, into not moving at all.

Dave quickly clasped on the cuff, ran to the front of the lighter, and fastened the chain to a prow bitt. Then he ran along the gunwale to the stem, threw off the rope, and waved to Dessour. The Frenchman started the launch forward, the towline straightened out, and they were off.

Thurston huddled in the bottom of the boat, making small, frightened noises to himself, hugging his knees.

Only once did he snap out of it. He threw his arms wide, despairingly, and the chain from his handcuffs ripped out the prow bitt, sent it clattering down to the bottom of the lighter. But Thurston never even noticed he was loose; he was too scared.

THE LAUNCH CAME alongside the *Lorelei's* landing platform. Dessour's blacks threw Dave's traps aboard. Then

Dessour put off again, maneuvering to bring the lighter in. As it went by the landing platform, Dave caught hold of the ladder and tied up. He ran along the gunwale again, Thurston snatching at him for comfort, but missing; got the chain, and went up, aboard the ship.

"Come on, Thurston!" he ordered. The captain met him at the top.

"You can't bring that aboard here!" he stormed. "I thought you had a cage."

"He's docile as a lamb," Dave promised. "Wouldn't hurt anything for the world."

Captain Dujarge tapped the dangling prow bitt at the end of the chain. "So I see."

A little man came dancing around the deck. "Weeth that I weel not sail. No, no—"

"A thousand times no," Dave said. "It's too late."

It was. To Thurston, the anchored freighter represented something steady in this world of shaking, rocking chaos. He had come up the landing ladder, briskly and meaning business, still carrying his trunk.

"Call the crew," Dave said, "and throw the beastie off."

"All right," Dujarge said. His coppery skin was a little paler. "But this will be five thousand dollars, mister, not three."

"Fifteen hundred's all I have with me," Dave said. "Another thirty-five hundred when we land."

The captain hesitated. The little man squealed. The captain looked at Thurston and shrugged. "Since we can't put him ashore anyway—" he said. "The forehold is empty. He can sleep there, take his sun in the forepeak. But he must stay chained."

"He will." Dave decided not to show the captain Thurston's escape act with the handcuffs.

He led the gorilla to the forepeak, chained him to a boom, then went back to the deck. "Whenever you're ready, captain."

The captain said, "All right. Meet Mr. Alan, who sails with us."

Mr. Alan's accent and color did not suggest such a Nordic name. He bowed politely, then turned to sweep his hat off to a woman who was coming onto the deck from the midstructure. "My secretary, Miss Ross, thees ees a feallow countryman, Mr. McNally."

The girl was young, less than twenty-five, and she had very black hair and very white skin.

She looked at Dave, then suddenly smiled. "Hello."

"Hello," Dave said.

"I—I like your little pet," the girl said.

Mr. Alan looked anxiously from one to the other.

Captain Dujarge said, "We might as well get the anchor up," and climbed the ladder to the bridge.

The anchor winch began rattling.

5

THE MATE TALKS

A WEEK LATER, Dave sat on the edge of the forepeak, and attempted to play the mouth organ that Nichols had left him. Down in the sun, sitting against a boom mast, Thurston contentedly pulled bananas off a stalk and munched them. He was tossing the skins into a neat pile beside one of his huge feet.

"He's a lamb," a lazy voice said behind Dave. "A nice little, woolly lamb." Miss Ross swung down to sit beside Dave; close beside him. She had on white slacks and a halter top.

"Scram, pal," Dave said good naturedly. "Mr. Alan doesn't seem to care for our association."

The girl's eyes played over Dave. "Scared, mister?" she drawled.

Dave chuckled, held the mouth organ a few inches from his mouth. He tapped the revolver at his belt. "Sure I'm scared. Babe, I'm bringing Broadway the sensation of the ages; something that would bring Barnum up from his grave. It's what I've looked for all my life; and it's enough for me just now. I don't want trouble. Any other time, I could mix into your affairs, and be glad to. But not just now, madam, not just now. You got yourself into this, and it's up to you to get out."

The girl did not take offense. "I know how it looks, Broadway," she said. "Only it isn't like that at all. He wanted to marry me. Me, all I wanted was to get back to New York. The show I was with blew up on the Riviera."

"And I suppose," Dave drawled, "that you thought you were sailing on a freighter for home. With Alan."

"His name isn't Alan. And—well, it wasn't a freighter at first. We started out on a liner, and I was being the Broadway wise girl, playing a middle-aged sucker for my passage home. Only—well, we transshipped, and—"

Dave blew a sour note on the mouth organ. He was trying hard to stay tough; he had to. This girl—well, he'd known a lot of them. Show girls, as decent as the next, but acting tough because it was the way to get along. Well, Mr. Alan was no stage door Johnny. The girl should have known better.

"He hasn't used force yet," the girl said, "because I know too much about what he was doing up in Somal—"

Dave said sharply, "Don't tell me, pal! I don't want anyone's secrets."

"But this is terrific, Broadway. We've been up in French Som—"

Dave pumped the mouth organ full of air, his fingers hitting all the Wrong notes, until Thurston put his hairy fingers in his ears. Dave laughed so hard he couldn't play any more. Thurston had finished his bananas, and was rising to his feet now. Slowly he gathered all the skins in his hands, and lumbered to the rail. Looking up, Dave saw the masts covered with Dujarge's polyglot crew of cutthroats; the antics of the gorilla had a sort of deadly fascination for them.

This was Thurston's afternoon amusement. He threw a banana skin overboard; the crowd of gulls that followed the ship came swarming. The big ape's hands moved like lightning among the birds; but he didn't get any that trip. He threw another skin, made another dive.

"This is marvelous," Mr. Alan's accented voice said. "Does he ever catch any of them?"

"Yeah, three or four an afternoon," Dave said. "He eats 'em, whole, too. But he likes the fun of catching the birds. I swear, that ape has a sense of humor."

"That ees a mooch overrated attribute," Mr. Alan said firmly. "Come, Miss Ross, there ees somet'ing for wheech I must speak to you."

"So long, Broadway," the girl said, rising. "See you later."

WHEN THEY WERE gone, Dave shook his head. There might be trouble in that direction. Alan was obviously a gun salesman, or some similar potentate; he had probably been up in French Somaliland doing something he shouldn't do on the borders of the still disturbed Ethiopia. Little brown men like that covered the globe. Dave had run into them often enough in his work, and they were never up to any good.

As for the girl—well, he was sorry for her. But—

The but was Thurston, still leaning over the rail like the fine, docile beast he was. Dave couldn't afford trouble this trip home. His belongings had been searched twice, either by the captain or by one of his freebooting crew, and he knew that it was only the fact that he had brought no money with him that kept him alive. He had foreseen that;

there were tramps rolling down the Seven Seas that were not a bit better than the old pirates, and this was one of them. Circumspect, but lawless as any murderer. Well, they were afraid of Thurston, which helped; and also, they were not likely to kill the ape, which Dave had at first feared, because they now realized how valuable he was, and that kind did not destroy money.

A pleasant trip. A man was a fool to go into this business of freak hunting. But it was in his blood—

And if they had quiet seas, and the girl didn't get scared, nothing might happen.

Only the girl was already scared, and the sea is never pleasant for a whole month. Dave rose, stretching. Strolling back to his cabin, he encountered the first mate, who was Chinese. The boatswain was a lascar, the chief engineer a Scot, the flag on the mast was the red ensign of the British Empire's commercial fleet. No doubt a man with a complete set of fingerprints of the crew of the good ship *Lorelei* would find an interested audience in any police station in the world.

The Chinese bowed to Dave.

"Been in my cabin?" Dave asked.

The first mate never understood anything he didn't want to. "Going to blow littly bit," he announced. "Blig monk', be he all the same Kokay?"

"O.K.," Dave said. He shrugged, and went by the politely bowing Oriental. He had chained his three guns to a steam pipe and padlocked them there; there were scratches on the padlock. He knelt in his cabin, frowning, looking at the padlock; if Dujarge had sent an engineer instead of a deck officer, those guns would be gone now.

Still frowning, Dave got the key out of his pocket, unlocked the guns. With his penknife as screwdriver, he removed a part here and there from the shotgun and the rifle; he rose, and went to the porthole. Sighing, he heaved the parts out the window. He could replace them in New York.

There remained his fine Mannlicher elephant gun. In all probability it was the only firearm on the ship capable of stopping Thurston. He knelt there, worrying. And as he knelt, he suddenly went forward, so that he had to put out a hand to steady himself.

The mate was right. It was beginning to blow a bit, the ship was rolling. He compromised by unscrewing the breeching of the elephant gun and putting it into his pocket. Then he chained the three guns back to the steampipe. Chuckling, he got out a bottle of brandy from his locked suitcase, and carried it up to the bridge. In the week that they had been sailing, it had become a custom for the passengers and the captain of the *Lorelei* to meet each evening before dinner on the bridge for a drink; it was his turn tonight to provide.

Miss Ross was leaning in one of the wings, with the captain's binoculars.

"What d'you see, pal?" Dave called.

She said, over her shoulder, "Cap'n there says we ought to sight land soon. St. Paul's Rocks."

"Yes," Dujarge said. "The rocks of Sao Paulo. Halfway between the Guineas and the Guianas. We're almost on them."

"Let's have a drink," Dave said.

The captain clapped his hands, and a steward appeared

with a tray of little glasses. McNally handed him the bottle, and the steward—a Portuguese-talking Negro—filled the liqueur glasses and handed them around.

Dave tasted his cognac, smiled, and looked out at the freshening sea.

"Captain," he said, "have you any narcotics in your drug chest?"

The captain's hand flashed to his hip suspiciously. "What? You accuse me of—"

"*Non, non, mon capitaine!*" Dave protested. "For the ape. If it blows too much. To make him sleep."

"Perhaps," the Canuck mulatto said smoothly, "something could be found. Of course, *m'sieur*, I would have to charge."

"I haven't got any more money with me," Dave pointed out. "Put it on the bill." He strolled over to the wing, where the cockney second mate was trying to pick up the rocks of Sao Paulo with his glasses. "Sight them yet?"

"I think so, sir. Hit's freshening hup a bit, though; 'ard to see ahead, sir." He handed over the glasses.

At the storm tossed and clouded seas ahead, Dave whistled. He said softly, to the cockney, "Trouble ahead. I wonder how Thurston's going to take the tossing?"

"There you 'ave me, sir. Some ipes tyke it lying down; some fights hit, sir."

"I know, I've transported small monkeys, and even chimps. Gorillas may be altogether different, though. I thought of getting some narcotic from the captain."

" 'E should be able to supply you with a touch of opium, sir."

Dave looked keenly at the second mate. He had never

much noticed him before, except that he was usually on duty on the bridge during the aperitif hour. "So that's the way it is?"

"Yes, sir." The mate squinted through his glasses. "Mine's liquor, sir. I lost my master's ticket that way."

"Why tell me?" Dave asked.

The mate was silent a moment. "They've figured out the ipe's worth real money, sir. They did plan to get what you could give for bringing him aboard, and then kill him."

"And now they plan on killing me, eh?" Dave grinned. "Come down to my cabin some time, mister. You and I might talk a little business."

"Hi thought as much, sir."

Dave turned back, saying, "Another drink, Alan, Miss Ross, Captain?" The steward poured the brandy. "If you could get me that dope, skipper? It's time I fed Thurston," Dave suggested.

"The rocks, Captain," the second mate cried.

"Halfway across the South Atlantic," Captain Dujarge said, drinking down his brandy. "I'll get you some opium, McNally, from the ship's stores." He went into the char-troom.

He walked to the chair he had vacated, sat down next to Mr. Alan. "Did you ever hear Lucienne Boyer sing?" he asked. "Or have you been in Paris?"

He and the swarthy man chatted lightly till a sailor brought Thurston's supper to Dave, and the captain appeared with the opium to dope him.

THE SHIP WAS already rocking and pitching, and Thurston huddled against the boom mast, whining to himself. He seemed glad to see Dave and made an effort to eat his supper. But he had hardly gotten down three mouthsful, when the ship gave a lurch, and Thurston fell over on his face and was seasick.

Afterwards, he lay on the canvas, still moaning. Dave found a woolen blanket and a tarpaulin, and covered the ape. Thurston grabbed his hand, and held it, and wouldn't let go. Dave squatted on the forepeak hatch, and prepared to ride out the storm. He shouted for a sailor to bring him supper, but none of them would come near Thurston.

After a while it was night, and the waves got higher. Dave thought of pneumonia, the scourge of the apes. If Thurston were to get sick—

A hand touched him on the shoulder. The show girl. Miss Ross, said: "I brought you some supper, Broadway. And the heel of the bottle of cognac you left on the bridge."

"You're not scared of the ape, anyway, pal," Dave said.

"He couldn't be any worse than that horror I'm traveling with. Why not give the poor monk a drink? He looks awful." Despite her cool words, her voice was shaking.

"It's an idea," Dave said. He uncorked the cognac, put the bottle between Thurston's heavy lips, and poured. The gorilla choked, but he swallowed. "Go get me another blanket, pal," Dave said. The girl went away.

She brought two back, and Dave laid one over Thurston, put the other on the hatch for a cushion. He and the girl sat shoulder to shoulder, looking down at the sleeping, moaning gorilla.

"Passed out," the girl said.

"You don't think much of me, do you, Broadway?" the girl asked. "Have you ever been a chorus girl stranded on the Riviera? You'd have taken passage with the old geezer, too. Give me a break, McNally."

"What kind of a break, kid? My job's to get Thurston here back to the States. I can't fool with anything else."

She sighed. "Well… There's the spig yelling. I got to go."

As she climbed up the ladder to the deck, Dave heard Alan saying: "What were you doing down there, with that, that monkey-nurse?"

And the girl said: "Nursing monkeys!"

The ship kept on rolling.

6

MUTINY

FAMILIARITY BREEDS SOME wonderful things. When the voice called: "Mr. McNally, Mr. McNally, sir!" Dave awoke and found he had, at some time during the night, crawled under the tarp with Thurston, and had been sleeping with his head on the ape's shoulder. Thurston still slept, with small snoring noises breaking out from his thick lips.

Dave crept across the forepeak, wet with the breaking seas, and scrambled up the ladder. The second mate, clad in oilskins, crouched there. "Hit's started, sir. The Chink went to your cabin to get you. You wasn't there."

"What's happened, Limey?"

"The capting told the crew to get you, sir. Hand the ipe. 'E's afryde the skykin'll stir the brute hup. The crew wouldn't do it, sir. They want the ipe for themselves. Then Mr. Halan hoffered them a thousand pound to knock you both hoff, and they agreed to hit. Seems Mr. Halan's a mite green-heyed, sir."

"Jealous, eh? He seems to have a lot of money, that little brown man."

"He's been smuggling harms into Somaliland, sir. Stirring hup trouble. Some says 'e's a Fascisti, tryin' to get the French to withdraw from Somali."

"Yeah, a guy like that would have dough....What'll we do, Limey?"

"Hif you lands the ipe in Hamerica, you're rich, sir. That's right? I can get two blokes from the engine room to throw hin with hus. You to p'y the three of hus two thousand pound when we land you. Catch hon, sir?"

"It's mutiny, isn't it?"

"This ship's a cooperative, sir. We chynge hit's name as hit hoccurs to us. The skipper'll not try hus, sir. Hit's every man for himself, haboard this packet."

"And if you kill Dujarge and the Chinese, you're captain, eh?"

In the dark, the cockney winked.

Just then, Dujarge bawled from the bridge: "McNally, Mr. McNally. Can you step up here a moment, please?"

"Coming!" Dave called, then whispered to the sailor: "Don't start anything till they jump me. I may be able to talk them out of this. And if they've taken my guns, don't let it worry you. The guns won't work."

He swung past the cockney and found the cargo mast, went up its steps to swing off onto the bridge. "Call me, Captain?"

The captain, the first mate, and Mr. Alan stepped out from one of the wings. "Come in the chartroom, McNally. We want to talk to you."

Dave followed them into the chartroom, his hand resting lightly on his hip, not far from the butt of the .45. "Yes, gentlemen?"

"We find it necessary to kill your gorilla," Dujarge said immediately. "The ship's having rough going, and it's getting rougher. If he gets disturbed, he may run amok, kill us all."

"I'll be responsible for him," Dave said steadily. "He's full of liquor, now. When he wakes up, I'll fill him up again. And so on, till the glass rises."

Mr. Alan said: "Where ees you got zat liquor?"

"Miss Ross was kind enough to bring it to me. She's the only person on this ship who isn"t afraid of Thurston."

"The ape goes!" Alan cried. "Eet ees I who charter the *Lorelei* first. I say so."

"So you can kill me," Dave said. "You won't do it while I'm protected by the ape."

"It is unfortunate," Dujarge put in, "but the poor Thurston must go. You will give us the breechblock of the Mannlicher. Ch'ien here will do the shooting."

Dave cursed him briefly, and clearly. His hand dropped to his belt.

The Chinese said: "No!" and whirled away from a chart table. He pointed Dave's shotgun at Dave's middle.

Dave grinned, and took a step towards the mate. The Chinese clicked both triggers. Nothing happened.

Dave put out a hand to grasp the shotgun barrel, to wrest it away from the mate, and the Chinese backed off, threw the barrel high, aimed a blow at Dave's head.

Glass crashed behind him, and the chartroom was filled with smoke and noise. The Chinese doubled up, his face no longer yellow, but red. The cockney second mate came through the shattered window, holding a Webley on Dujarge and Alan. "Go hover them, Mr. McNally. Get their guns."

As the captain and the diplomat raised their hands,

Dave took a gun from each. Dave shoved them into his pockets, felt the breeching of the Mannlicher. "Where's my elephant gun? I need it."

The captain sneered silently.

The mate said: "Hi've been promoted once, skipper, Hi' don't mind another."

"This is mutiny, Mr. Whitstun." The captain's face was pale.

"An 'ow did you get to be capting, except by conkin' Larrabie?"

"That's right, Nick!" Dujarge bawled. Whitstun half turned, and Dujarge grabbed Alan's wrist, and jerked him to the top of the stairs leading down to the captain's cabin. They disappeared, and a door slammed below.

At the same time, a rough voice yelled from the bridge: "Mister Whitstun. The ape's loose!"

The cockney paled, looked at Dave with consternation. Dave shoved past him, past the bridge where a stoker held a gun on the helmsman and the lascar third mate. He swung out on the ladder of the boom mast, and peered down through the spray.

Thurston was standing in the middle of the cargo hatch, water splashing against his chest. As Dave watched, the big gorilla raised his arms, and he saw that he had broken the chain.

Thurston bawled something in a voice that was half an anguished shriek, and half a bark of rage. He beat his chest with his mighty fists.

Whitstun leveled the revolver on the bridge rail, and took aim.

"No," Dave bawled, over the noise of the storm and the

enraged ape. "No! That'll just make him mad, you can't stop a gorilla with a revolver bullet. I'll go down."

He clambered down the ladder, sweat making his hands slick on the rungs.

Halfway down, a white face over the bridge's edge and a high voice stopped him. "Come back," the girl cried.

That was funny enough to make Dave grin. He went on down.

For a moment, as though even the elements wanted to see what was going to happen, the ship was still, poised on a wave. The ship was still, and so was the mighty gorilla's voice.

"Take it easy, Thurston," Dave shouted, and went down the rest of the way. As his foot groped for the bottom rung, he was snatched off the ladder, and seized in a pair of powerful, hairy arms that knocked the wind out of him, and nearly broke his ribs.

Thurston rubbed his huge brown face against Dave's and whimpered, miserably.

Dave wriggled, tried to get loose, but the gorilla clung to the one familiar thing in this pitching, watery world in which he had awakened with the taste of liquor stale in his mouth.

McNally managed to get his arm loose, but that was all. His feet did not touch the hatch.

A spotlight was turned on them from the bridge, and the showgirl yelled: "Here, Dave." Something hurtled at him from her hands, and he caught it with his fingertips, it was a bottle of cognac.

"He might," the girl screamed, "just as well be drunk as the way he is."

Dave fumbled the cork out of the bottle, held it to Thurston's lips. The ape tasted, coughed, then, presumably, remembered how this stuff had made him feel better before. He grabbed for the bottle, and Dave fell to the hatch.

7

THE BIG TIME

DAVE CLIMBED THE boom ladder to the bridge again. The third mate had disappeared; Whitstun was directing the helmsman himself. "Hi've bought hoff 'arf the crew, sir," he said. "The Chinaman was the one they was afryde hof. Not Dujarge."

"How's the barometer?" Dave asked. "I can't keep that monkey drunk all the time. It may kill him."

"You sets a lot of store on that ipe, sir, and that's a fact," Whitstun said. "Clear seas by mornin', Hi reckon."

"Fair enough. Where's Miss Ross?"

"Gone below."

Dave started to take the rear way down, when the mate stopped him. "What's that in your 'and, sir?"

"Handcuffs. I figure to fasten Alan and the captain together if I can catch them."

"Orf the ipe, sir?" Whitstun's eyes rolled.

"Sure. He took them off."

"The crew may not tyke that kindly, sir."

"I'm paying this crew enough to make them like anything," Dave barked. He made to go past.

"We hain't seen the color of your money, Mr. McNally."

"So now that starts," Dave stormed. "Look, is the radio man on your side?"

"He is."

"Come in the radio room with me, then, and I'll send off a message to Miami."

"Whitstun told the helmsman to "Keep 'er as she is," and followed Dave. The American sat down in the radio shack and wrote out a message to Jacob Loeb in New York.

"Have A-1 attraction landing at Miami within two weeks. Meet me there with strong cage and fifteen grand in cash." He handed the message over. "Send that. Ask for confirmation. If you want to know who Jake Loeb is, wire anybody you know in New York."

"I used to play in an orchestry," the radio man said, scratching his curly hair. "I know him."

"Got money?" asked Whitstun.

"A mintful," the radio man said. "If he answers this right, the monkeynurse here is O. K, with me."

"That does it, then," Whitstun said. "Send it. Now, we—"

The girl rushed into the room. Her blouse had been torn away from one shoulder; there was a scratch on one side of her face. "They're in his cabin," she screeched, "the captain and the little twerp. Breaking out the hand grenades."

"The—" Dave's face went pale. "They can't use those. They'll rip holes in this ship. They—"

There was a dull roar outside. Dave knocked Whitstun down in his rush for the door.

A HOLE GAPED in the forehatch. It was too far forward to have hurt the ape; but a sudden clearing of the spray as the prow went up showed Dave, the captain and Alan crouched behind the anchor winches forward, trying to get another pitch.

"Thurston!" Dave yelled.

The ape swung around groggily; the bottle in his hand was empty. The captain heaved another bomb, then, and Dave shut his eyes. But the explosion was delayed for moments; and then it was just a shower of water. Either the bomb had bounced off Thurston and overboard, or he had pitched it.

But the ape was mad now, and he had something to vent his drunken, pent-up spleen on. Dave gasped as the gorilla grabbed up his magic-chest and started forward.

McNally could not fire now; Thurston was between him and the winches. He started down the cargo mast ladder to help his gorilla; then stopped. Something had infuriated the ape; he shoved his box high over his head and heaved it forward towards the foam-covered spray.

It was all confusion then. A sheet of blinding flame, and Thurston going backward. Then the smoke clearing, and Thurston sitting there quietly, for a moment, then starting back for them. And one winch engine gone overboard, and a section of rail with it.

The girl sobbed, "The little twerp, the poor little twerp!"

"He ees all right!" Alan's voice said.

They whirled. The little brown man stood in the chartroom door. "The captain, he went to get the ape," Alan said. "I went to get the ape's master. Here I am." The rifle in his hands was not Dave's; but it was leveled at Dave's chest.

"I wouldn't," McNally said steadily. "I wouldn't, Alan. Because the captain didn't get Thurston; Thurston got him. Dujarge threw a grenade the same time Thurston threw that trunk; the trunk was heavier, and there's no more Dujarge. I wouldn't shoot at me, Alan; if you do, there'll be no one to control Thurston."

"I'll take my chances. There ees another grenade in my case, eet weel do—"

The radioman rushed from his shack yelling, "Look. Lookee what I just picked up. She's only a couple of miles behind us, and coming fast. She—"

Alan turned his head, lowered his rifle, and Dave's foot came up. The rifle went off, but it damaged nothing but the canvas over the bridge. Then Dave's fist clicked on the little man's chin, and Alan went over backwards.

The rifle skidded out of his hand.

Dave bent over, snapped the cuffs on Alan.

Whitstun said to the radio man, "Nice work. Did you really pick up something?"

"Yeah. There's a French gunboat coming up on us at thirty knots. With a warrant for the guy we called Mr. Alan. He's—"

"I know who he is. But they can't do anything to us. We're flying the British duster."

The radio man looked at Whitstun, and said, "We better take it down. They radioed that Lloyd's has told them the real *Lorelei* was wrecked at sea two years ago. The derelict's just been found."

"We're sunk—" Whitstun said. "Put 'er about, 'ead back for Africa. Get two men over the side, and repaint the name. Make it the—the Hoboken. Run hup han Hamerican—"

Dave stepped in. "Let it go. You'll never get away that way. Look, I don't know what you've done, but I don't care, either. And I don't imagine the French will, if they get Alan. Let me talk."

HALF AN HOUR later, Lieutenant Delevan of the French Navy came aboard, while the gunboat and the freighter wallowed in the trough of the sea. At the sight of Thurston, who had managed to get into the chartroom before he passed out, he whistled. "We touched at Joffre," he told Dave in good enough English. "I heard about this—this creature. I hardly believed. Well, all aboard this ship, they are under arrest; except you, Mr. McNally. If you wish, we can take you to Paramaribo; we are bound for Cayenne, anyway. There you should be able to get a boat for the United States."

"Sure, only—" Dave winked. "Why pinch the crew here. Dujarge is dead; and the rest of these men had only shipped for the voyage."

Delevan looked interested. "You mean—"

"One man—say a little brown man—could go to Cayenne without trial. His—government—would never dare make inquiries. But a whole boatload of men—"

"There is that," Delevan said. "There is that. And you, *m'sieur*. You will do what with the ape? We cannot get him aboard our gunboat, I fear—"

"He's passed out," Dave said. "Give that monkey a bottle of cognac and he'll go any place, asleep. But I'll tie his hands and feet."

As they were shoving off, Thurston's head pillowed on Dave's knee, the girl's face appeared at the top of the ladder. "Wait for baby," she chirped.

But two days later, speeding for South America at thirty knots, the storm died, and the sun came out. Thurston sat chained to the mast of the gunboat eating bananas for the worst hangover in simian history. And Dave, leaning on the rail, heard light heels tapping on the deck, and said, over his shoulder, "Hi, Toots."

The girl stopped, said quickly, "Cut out that Toots stuff, Mr. McNally. I'm a lady. Fifty million Frenchmen," she added, "can't be wrong."

She walked on, and a minute later, following her, came a neat little group of gold braided officers, eying each other suspiciously. The one with the beard had freshly combed it, and even parted it up the middle.

Dave went over and patted Thurston on the shoulder. "We're still heading for the big time, kid. All of us."

THE VALLEY OF MAGIC MEN

There was a giant magician in that lonely lamasery who could read the souls of men—and Dave McNally had to bring-him-back-alive

1

THE SOUL-SEEING GIANT

THE ENGLISHMAN STARED at the card, and then at Dave McNally. "But really," he said. "I don't understand. Expeditions, yes; anyone knows what expeditions are. But amusements? I don't quite—"

Dave bit the lining of his cheek to keep from laughing. "The amusements," he explained patiently, "are what come out of the expeditions. I go on an expedition, see? Then I come back with an amusement. Like, one time, I made a trip to Africa; I came back with a performing gorilla, Thurston the Ape-Man, and he is now being exhibited by Jake Loeb all over the United States."

The British Resident scratched his head. "But the amusements. It says on your card, Expeditions & Amusements. Now, where do the amusements come in."

"The gorilla is an amusement," Dave said. "An attraction, a—"

"I say," cried the Englishman, "you're pulling my leg, aren't you? I mean, all this stuff about amusements and gorillas and so forth. Everyone knows there are no gorillas in Thibet. Hal Smithers put you up to this, now didn't he?"

Dave leaped to his feet. "D'you know old Smithers? Say,

it's a small world after all. I had no idea you were a friend
of dear old Hal's."

"Oh, but of course," the Resident said. "Hal and I were
at public school together. Are you a friend of his? I suppose
you met him in Singapore."

"We had a fine time in Singapore together," Dave said

*McNally stared
at the Abbot*

gravely. "He wouldn't let me stay at a hotel, made me stop
at his house with him."

"Oh, well," the Resident said, "if you're a friend of Hal's,
that's different."

"Dear old Hal," Dave sighed, and watched, with glitter-

ing eyes, the Englishman sign the papers permitting one Dave McNally, an American citizen, to recruit porters and journey into Thibet.

"Mention me to Smithers when you write," Dave said, and scooped up the papers. He got out of there, wondering if he had ever met anyone named Smithers in Singapore.

One obstacle out of the way. It should be no trouble to get porters; the Thibetans would work for very little. As for mountain passes, snowdrifts, landslides and superstitious natives, he'd cross those bridges when he came to them. The main thing was to find a guide who knew where the Lao-Chatze Valley was.

THE MAN WHO ran the labor market was an Eurasian. He was very glad to see Dave. "Oh, yes sir, we rent you portahs.

Yes sir, very good men, work for American before. You go to hunt the animals, isn't it, yes sir? I rent you portahs, spottahs, trackas. All first class men, you do not have to pay them; we do that. Half now, half when they bring you back safely. That way you are, yes sir, in no dangah. You comprehend?"

"Oh, quite," Dave carefully read the contract extended to him, signed it, paid over money. "All right, we start tomorrow, then. I'll be ready to examine the outfit tonight." He stood up, took three paces towards the door, and, with his back turned, said, in what he hoped was a casual voice: "Your guide will know the way to the Lao-Chatze Valley, won't he?"

It hadn't worked. The Eurasian jumped up. "Oh, no, yes sir. There are no animals in the Lao-Chatze, yes sir. Our gentlemen they never hunt there. Oh, never. You must try the shoulder of Mount—"

"But I want to go to the Lao-Chatze," Dave said.

"Always our men go around there, yes sir. No, yes sir, they do not know the way."

"If they know how to go around it, they know how to get to it," Dave pointed out. "They'll take me there, or the deal is off."

"Oh, but yes sir, the Lao-Chatze is very holy, yes sir. There is an abbot there—"

"Yes. An abbot?" Dave concealed the eagerness of his voice. "You said an abbot?"

"The head of the Lao-Chatze Monastery, yes sir. I do not know about him."

Dave led him on. "Isn't he a giant of some sort? I heard—"

"Yes sir, he is very tall. But all the lamas of the Lao-Chatz are tall. Many of them over eight feet, which, I hear is the height of the Abbot. But, yes sir, it is not that. He—thees is all superstitious native tommyrot, yes sir, of course—he can see souls, yes sir." The labor man was hushing his voice despite himself.

"See souls? What do you mean?"

"He—he can look at you, yes sir, and know what you are thinking, what you really are. He does not see bodies, yes sir; he sees souls."

Dave said: "Oh, I see."

"The natives are very afeared of him, yes sir. They will not go into the valley. He is most frightfully holy."

"He must be." Dave looked at the cowed Asiatic who just a moment before, had been such a sleek European clerk. There was certainly something about this lama of the Lao-Chatze Valley that impressed people.

Nevertheless, Dave McNally intended to bring the Abbot back with him. Show business was plenty tough these days, and you had to keep giving the public more and more. A giant who was a Thibetan monk, and who also was a genuine and convincing mind reader seemed like the right number. The public was fed up with Hindu mystics; it was not too lenient with giants anymore. But the combination—

The clerk remembered business, and cried: "Yes sir, you must promise, if you go to the Lao-Chatze, you will not attempt to coerce your porters in with you. You must go alone."

"I promise," Dave said, and left. He went over to the English Club and had a drink with an Italian oilman and

two Dutch camel traders. Gradually the eerie feeling he
had gotten in the office left him.

2

TONKA

A MULE COULD not have made it. He would have been too long to get around the curves. A donkey might have gotten through, but not with a pack on his back. But the Thibetan porters swung along merrily on the two-foot shelf path, and never stopped for breath, though the heavy *kiltas* on their backs—baskets not unlike those used by an Adirondack guide—were nearly as large as they, themselves.

Below them the birds soared and wheeled in the sun. The gorge was a thousand feet deep here, and getting deeper; the path that twisted and clung to the slopes of the Thibetan foothills rose about one foot in twenty.

The head porter, who was also the game spotter, went first, kicking loose stones idly out into the gorge with his foot. The path was far from smooth; but as each man came along, he shoved the more obvious rolling pebbles out and down, so that by the time Dave, who brought up the rear, got there, the danger from stepping on anything loose was minimized. Lloyd's of London, always sporting, might have sold him a thousand dollar life insurance policy for five hundred dollars, spot cash.

His fingers were raw from catching at projecting knobs of stone to ease himself around the worst corners. The

Thibetans scorned this; when they came to a corner where the generous two feet of the ledge narrowed to a miserly one foot, they turned their faces out and went along sideways, leaning against the weight of their packs as a sailor leans against the wind.

Dave noticed that the Thibetan way of going seemed to be to move the foot only an inch from the ground at a time. This shuffle cleared the path as a man went along; it also made the ankles ache, the back groan, the shoulders squeal with pain.

It was bitter cold, but exertion kept making him sweat; and though they were only in what Thibetans call the foothills, the altitude had him dizzy.

Suddenly the spotter cried: "Hup."

With one accord the porters flung themselves on their faces, their baskets on top. The spotter kneeled and pointed like a bird-dog. Far above them, posed on a rock, Dave saw a Thibetan goat, his long and curling horns catching the rays of the sun.

HE BROUGHT DOWN his rifle, pumped in a cartridge, and aimed carefully. He threw an extra hundred feet in for luck; mountain distances were notoriously deceptive. His finger slowly tightened on the trigger, even as he thought that, should he hit the goat, there was very little chance of catching the body before it went into the gorge below him. But his contract with the labor company said that he must shoot game to help feed the porters.

He fired. The crash echoed and reechoed across the gorge; it seemed as though a whole company of sportsmen had discharged their weapons.

The goat threw up his head, and shook it. Then slowly, he began to sink to his knees.

The two rear porters, who were also game trackers by profession, had already slipped their *kilta* straps, and were bounding up the slope over them; a slope that seemed not merely perpendicular, but almost overhanging. They worked together, one man lying down while the other climbed over him, then the second one pulling the first after him.

They were only fifty feet below the goat when the animal's knees hit the rock, and he rolled over.

The trackers promptly split up, one to the right, one to the left. The goat rolled, fell, came tumbling down—into the arms of one of the trackers. They brought the body back.

The head porter whipped out a two-foot knife and deftly quartered the animal, split it up amongst various carriers. He looked at Dave, " 'ead or 'orns, sah?" Like many Thibetans he had learned his English from British soldiers on shooting leave.

"Just the horns," Dave said.

The head man trimmed them off, rubbed the base with salt, shoved them into a *kilta* so that they rode above the carrier's back. Dave grinned. He was no trophy collector, but to pass up the horns would make these men suspicious; if they knew whom he was going to see, they would surely turn back.

They went ahead again, the men talking and chuckling amongst themselves. The leader pressed himself into an embrasure, and let the pack train go ahead of him so he could talk to Dave.

"Me say so, sah, that pretty damn shot. Men pleased."

"Oh, is that what they're talking about? Yes, I've been shooting all my life."

"Men say, we eat well, this time out, sah."

"Good. When do we camp?"

"Pletty soon, sah. After Tonka, no wattah; we camp by Tonka tonight."

"O.K."

DAVE WATCHED HIM winding in and out of the porters to take up the lead again, squeezing by where there had been room only for one. Dave McNally would have liked to shut his eyes, but he couldn't without falling off the ledge. For the first time it occurred to him that this was a fool sort of a trip; he had to persuade a Thibetan to come back to the United States with him. Dave spoke no Thibetan. And there was no reason to suppose that the lama, highly educated though he might be, would speak English.

Well, in this business, you couldn't plan too far ahead, or you never got started. It would have taken months to learn Thibetan. And he couldn't trust an interpreter in a delicate matter like this.

He settled down to walking some more. He hoped that in time he would get used to climbing endlessly along a ledge wide enough to hold a small coffee pot.

At three in the afternoon, the road suddenly started going down, and a half an hour later they hit a flattened out spot; what was called a valley in the foothills. Tiny cows, no bigger than burros, grazed precariously on small meadows sloped almost as sharply as the trail had been. There were two huts, one large, one small.

"This Tonka," the head porter said to Dave. "These men

home now." He pointed at the four carriers who usually walked behind him.

Dave looked at the two huts. "Four families here?"

"Oh, no, sah. Only one family. One wife, five husban'. You see, sah, hill people very backward."

"Yeah, I see." Dave watched with amusement while the wife of Tonka came out and unceremoniously boxed the ears of her four returning husbands. The fifth one was evidently a tiny spot on the hills, out watching the cows.

Three or four children, all small but varied, ran around underfoot and watched their mother hit their fathers. "Quite a system," Dave said. "That babe sure couldn't get five husbands any other place in the world." She was about the dirtiest woman he had ever seen.

Having finished chastising her spouses, the woman of Tonka came and bowed before Dave, holding a leg of the goat he had shot in her hands.

"She says," the head porter interpreted from a mess of clicks and chuckles, "that you are a very fine shot. She hopes you will kill well and often, so that she may have meat from the trip."

"Just so she isn't proposing, it's O.K. by me," Dave said. "Get my tent up, will you?"

"Yes, sah." The porters fell to work putting up his tent; the woman went back into her hut and began screaming at the children, who ran around collecting sticks for a fire.

Dave flopped on his folding cot, regarding the bright, hard sun through the canvas. He was pooped. He turned over on his side to get some sleep when an object on the floor of the tent—the dirt floor—caught his eye. He reached over, picked it up.

It was the burnt stub of a paper match. He rubbed it between his fingers; it was fresh. He called the game spotter. "Portah, portah!"

The man came in, grinning and bowing. Dave said: "There've been white people here just lately. Last night, today."

"I find out, yes, sah!" The man bowed and went out again. Dave could hear him chattering to the woman. He came back: "Yes, sah, you are very smart. Party left here this morning. They are shooting, sah!"

"English?" Dave held his breath while the man went outside and chattered some more. All he needed was a party of English officers to gum things up. The English did not like the idea of people monkeying with the natives' religion in this, their protectorate. It started trouble.

The porter stuck his head in. "No, sah. They French, the woman say."

"O.K., pal. Wake me for dinner." That was all right. Probably some gang from a museum out shooting for skins and heads to mount. Nuts with it—he'd get some sleep.

When he woke up, it was only to eat goat stew and drink a peg of whisky. He was not long out of the tropics, and the cold and the altitude bothered him. He would not be surprised if he had picked up a touch of malaria in Africa that last time.

3

THE BARREN LAND

DAVE MCNALLY AWOKE in the morning with a confused remembrance of having heard noises in the night, as though someone had arrived at Tonka. Probably a dream. He yelled for water and sponged himself in his tent. The water was shockingly cold.

Tea—coffee was too much trouble on the trail—canned biscuit and canned cornbeef hash made his breakfast, while the children of Tonka looked on admiringly, and then squabbled over the empty tins. The porters were already fed and loading.

Dave, scrubbing his teeth after breakfast, went along the line to check the *kiltas*. He had had trouble before with stuff left behind that was badly needed the next day.

He stopped, suddenly, shook the toothbrush that he had been using while he walked and started over again. Well, maybe he was screwy, but he didn't think so.

The day before there had been eight *kiltas*, including the two light ones carried by the trackers. Now there were ten. He motioned to the head porter to have the men unsling and unpack. He had been used once to smuggle arms to back country tribes; it would be done again to him. But everything in the packs was his own; in fact it had been packed so neatly that it now seemed impossible that it could ever have fitted into eight baskets.

The head porter told seven lies before Dave got the truth out of him. Two porters had deserted the caravan ahead. Since they had no rifles, and since their home was miles away, they had asked to join this packtrain, in exchange for meat on the way home. "They no ask dollah, sah. They work for food, no costa you money."

Dave waved that aside. "Why did they quit their jobs? Is that the way you boys are going to do to me if the going gets tough?"

"Oh, no, sah. Thibetan man only quit, you beat him. Only wife can beat man." That was funny, even with a problem on his hands that he couldn't read. Dave McNally didn't like unreadable problems on the trail. "Who beat them?"

"Clazy woman, sah. She plenty wild."

"Woman?" Dave turned this over. "Say, what is this caravan ahead?"

The porter shrugged, and indicated with raised eyes that all Europeans who did not shoot game were incomprehensible to him. Dave said: "O.K., get them moving."

THE CARAVAN TOOK off, the woman of Tonka waving them good-bye. Dave noticed another change in the lineup; the husband who had been watching the herd the day before was now carrying a *kilta,* and one of the porters was staying home. That meant nothing; the contract had undoubtedly been made out with the family.

With the load distributed among ten *kiltas* instead of eight, the porters moved faster. It occurred to Dave that, unless their paths branched, they would overtake the party ahead pretty soon.

He stopped, waving to the porters to go ahead. Squatting on a rock, he got out his map, studied it. The Lamasery of Lao-Chatze was three day's travel, by the map; they had been a little short on their first day, Tonka was only a quarter of the distance out. Now—

A buzzard swooped down from overhead, passed within six feet of Dave's outstretched hand, and dove on into the gorge below, crying out as it went. Dave went to the edge of the narrow trail, and looked down.

There was no bottom. This early in the morning the gorge was filled with mist; wisps of it floated up as the sun hit it. He threw a pebble, and it seemed like five minutes before the noise of its landing came back to him. He turned, and looked up.

A thousand feet above his head an outcropping of rock kept him from seeing the top of the mountain around whose shoulder they were making their tortuous way.

There was no noise any place in the world but the faint crying of birds. No bird sang in these Himalayas; they cried. There was one school of native thought that believed that Himalayan birds were the lost souls of men, doomed forever to haunt the loneliness of the world's tallest mountains.

Nothing grew on the ledge, only above was there a little heather-like weed clinging to the rocks.

A feeling of remoteness, of almost horrid loneliness filled Dave McNally. He was used to the back tracks of the world. He was as at home in the jungles of the Amazon or the swamps of equatorial Africa as on the sidewalks of Times Square. But the jungles of the Amazon were a joke; where explorers penetrated and wrote books about their daring, Dave had found towns of five thousand Indi-ans and half-breeds, and had held joyous and noisy battle with them over the sale of monkeys and parrots and snakes and jungle cats. And as for Africa—you were lucky if you could avoid Englishmen who shaved every morning or Frenchmen who carried chessboards and mustache curlers.

BUT THIS WAS different. This was barren as the Sahara had not been barren. There was nothing to bring man here, either modern man or the primitives of the jungles. A few huts like Tonka, inhabited by a dying and race suiciding people; and the monasteries, the abodes of the Red Lamas, who preached what was called the "purest," most ascetic, religion in the world; the religion that held out little hope to its communicants, but said that by disciplining the body and training the mind, one might, in another thousand reincarnations arrive at: nothing—a state in which one was a pure thought and no more.

Or that was Dave's conception. He—

He brought himself to with a jerk and was afraid. Noth-ing around him but mist, nothing below him but mist, nothing above him but the rocks. He was alone—alone, in a world as coldly inhospitable as an operating room.

He scrambled to his feet and ran along the ledge after his porters, shoving the map into his pocket. His foot caught on a loose pebble, his ankle turned a little, and he tottered, one leg almost over the brink. Then he dropped flat to his face on the trail, pressing his body down, hugging each little knob of rock as though it was all there was between him and—nothingness.

His lungs took in the diamond-bright air in deep gulps, and his body shook.

Then after a moment, he rolled over, sat up, and got a bottle out of the breast pocket of his shooting coat. He took ten grains of quinine, washed them down with water from his canteen, and walked easily on after his caravan, his fine, high powered rifle swinging on his shoulder.

Jungle fever was a bad thing to take into the mountains he told himself gravely.

He caught the tail end of the caravan and, before they stopped for lunch, shot two more goats and a deer. Somehow or other, the sight of the animals and the clear crack of his rifle cheered him up. If a goat could stand it, he could.

4

THE RUSSIANS

THEY CAMPED FOR lunch where a stream of water pierced the rock and tumbled across the trail. One of the porters broiled the kidneys of the animals Dave had shot on a spit, and presented them to him, alternating them with squares of tender venison. The food was very good. He broke out a can of tomatoes from a *kilta* and ate them, too. There are no vegetables on the trail.

He waited until the men had eaten and were filling their pipes with crude tobacco. Then he called the head porter: "George! Hey, George."

The man came up, bowed, said: "My name 'Enry."

"All right, Henry. How far ahead do you think that other party is now?"

"Not far, sah. Their fire still warm when we make ours."

"Think we'll have trouble with them?"

Henry shrugged. "You good shot with rifle, sah. No trouble."

"I get it. People who beat coolies don't tackle people who use rifles. Right?"

"To a T, sah," Henry was full of linguistic surprises.

"O.K. Whenever you're ready to start, then."

They took off a half an hour later. But the sun was slanting under Dave's helmet before he realized that they were about to overtake the gang ahead; the sign was that the two rear coolies, the porters who had deserted the other party, suddenly stopped and squeezed into an embrasure in the cliff to let Dave get ahead of them. According to the English rules for traveling, this was bad etiquette; the boss in the Himalayas always comes last. But under the circumstances; Dave decided they were right.

Then they rounded a curve, and came upon them. Looking back, Dave saw that the two deserters had set their *kiltas* down and disappeared. The Thibetan is as agile as a mountain goat.

There were three of them. To the Thibetans, they might be French, but they didn't look it to Dave. Well, maybe the thin man with the beard was. But the woman was too dark; a Slav of some sort. And the fat man who sat with his shoes off, ruefully rubbing his wool-stockinged feet, had an Oriental cast of features. Not Chinese or Japanese, but something East of Suez.

DAVE WENT FORWARD, raising his hand in salute, but not putting the gun down from the sling on his shoulder. His coolies were unloading, the baskets making dull thuds on the ground but they were not unpacking.

"Hello," Dave said. It sounded a little flat.

"*Parlez-vous francias?*" asked the thin man.

"No," Dave said, more or less truthfully. The French he spoke would not have been claimed by the Academie. But he understood the language all right. "I'm American," he said. He had been watching their faces. They seemed relieved to hear that he was not a French-speaker, and not interested at all to know he was an American.

"I used to live in America," the girl said. Her voice was guttural, but unaccented to a New York ear. "I worked in a factory in New Jersey."

"Yeah? I'm a New Yorker," Dave said. He squatted, the butt of his rifle touching the ground. "My head porter tells me this is the only water in the next three hours march. I guess we'll have to camp together tonight."

"All right," the girl said. "You stay on that side of the clearing, we'll use this one."

"That's O.K. with me, toots," Dave said.

He turned, shouted an order at 'Enry, and then sat down with his back against the cliff. Henry sent a coolie over with a bottle of brandy. Dave coolly surveyed the other three foreigners, then unscrewed the metal top of the bottle, poured some liquor into it, and sipped it. He recorked the bottle and set it down beside him. T'ell with 'em. If they wanted to act snooty, nine thousand miles from no place, that was their worry. A man didn't go into the side show supply business because he craved a crowd around him all the time.

He watched his men pitch his tent, lay out his blankets, build a fire. Eight porters for one white man was ridiculous, he knew; but most of his life was spent in the wilderness, and he liked his comfort. The foreigners were setting up their own tent. There was no meat in evidence on their side of the clearing, but already Dave's cook was scoring the sides of a haunch of venison, no larger than a spring lamb, with salt and a knife, tendering it up for the master's dinner. Another coolie was making gravy in a tin from the tougher parts of the deer. Dave called Henry over and told him to get some dried mushrooms from the food *kilta* and add them to the gravy.

He took another drink of brandy, and sniffed the fine odors from the cooking fires. His coolies were eating stew again. They *liked* goat stew.

Dave felt just as good as he lead felt bad the night before.

The thin man's lips were trembling, and he was tugging at the wisp of goatee.

Dave called the gun porter over, asked him for his twenty-two. There was still light; he began taking pots at the birds that flew over the gorge. Something on the air, something in the feel of his muscles made him feel cruel, agile, as sleek as a mountain lion.

Nuts with the high-hat devils. A side show man wasn't good enough for them, eh. He grinned as he saw the girl apportioning out hard tack and bully beef. Bunch of tenderfeet! Helping the coolies when they should have been sitting back, resting. Coolies were used to their own country, it was no strain on them to work.

They must be rotten bad shots, too, not to have any game for dinner. Hell with 'em!

THERE WAS NO doubt in Dave's mind that the other party had nothing at all to do with any museum. Museum expeditions knew what they were doing. And what would they bring back for the collection, if they couldn't shoot?

He caught the fat man's eye, then, and the half-grin faded off Dave McNally's face. When the gun porter had brought him the .22, he had unloaded the other guns.

Besides the game rifle that he carried and the .22 he was playing with now, there was the fine Mannlicher elephant gun that was his pride, and the two shotguns. The fat man was looking at them where they lay in their leather cases. He wanted those guns, there was no question about it.

Idly, tauntingly, Dave swivelled the .22 around until it pointed at the fat man. Fatty must have felt the force of Dave's eyes on him; he turned, saw the gun, dropped his eyes. Dave let the gun pass on, as though it were an accident.

Dave called: "Henry!" When the porter came up, he said: "If you want to give those other porters some of your stew, it's O.K. with me. I've plenty of cartridges, I'll get you another goat tomorrow."

"Yes, sah. You are indeed a fine shot, sah." In Thibetan, Henry called over to the other camp. One of the porters from there brought a native saucepan, and Henry filled it with stew. The four coolies who were working for the girl's party fell upon it ravenously, grabbing up big chunks of the goat's meat with their fingers, wolfing it down, then passing the saucepan from mouth to mouth to drink the gravy.

The cook-coolie brought over Dave's tin plate and knife and fork. Tender slices of mountain venison floated in the mushroom gravy. Dave helped himself to another thimbleful of brandy, and started to eat.

The thin man could hardly control himself now.

Dave decided the game had gone far enough. He called over to the girl: "If you and the professors want to chow with me, there's plenty for all of us."

They held a conversation in something that was French, but even worse French than Dave's. He tried to place it, couldn't.

Then they came over, meekly. All they had said was: "Comrades, shall we share with this bourgeoisie?" and some chatter about Dave's undoubtedly being a spy, but he had them, now. Russians, Communists. But they weren't like any latter-day Communists he had met out of Russia. They were too furtive, and too mousy at the same time. With all Russia to draw from, the Kremlin would not be likely to send three such indoor babies on a spying or trouble-making trip through the high Himalayas.

They settled down around him, looking up at him. "Three plates for my friends, Henry," Dave called.

They ate, but the fat man's eyes kept drifting towards the guns. Dave said to the girl: "Russians, aren't you?"

"White Russians, yes. Not these pigs of Communists!" There was fervor in her tone.

"I'm not trying to pry into your business," Dave said, leisurely. The dinner had been very good. "I'm in the amusement trade myself. Collecting animals for sideshows. It takes me plenty of places where I wouldn't be nosy and get out alive."

"We're collecting for a museum in Paris," the girl said.

"O.K. with me sister." Suddenly, he was irritated again. "Only—tell your fat pal that I need those guns. And that, besides them, I have a revolver, and I always sleep with it in my hands. And you might add," he said, "that I've been in places where a gun was worth its weight in 24 carat gold, and I've never lost one yet."

In pure New Yorkese, she answered: "Tough guy, aren't you?"

His anger dissolved. "Sorry. Kind of poor hospitality, from one old American to another. The altitude makes me kind of scrappy, though. Tea?"

With their tea they became rude. They chattered among

themselves. One of them, the thin one, evidently couldn't understand Russian, because when the girl and the fat boy spat the Slavonic accents at each other, they seemed to interpret to him afterwards in their doggerel French.

But the word for American is almost undisguisable. He caught it several times. Abruptly the girl turned to him: "Where do you live in New York?"

Night was coming down over the Himalayas. Behind the Russians, the coolies were giggling about something. Dave said: "What the devil! If you people want to know about me, ask me. Or let it go. Only if that fat pal of yours—and I've said it before—starts anything, he's going to be sorry."

"You are a New Yorker, though? It's important that we know."

"Born in a theatrical boarding house on 38th. My office is on Times Square, here's my card, I live in a hotel when I'm home, and if you muggs are through drinking my tea, I'm going to turn in."

They didn't bother to apologize. They carried the card away as though it were valuable. Dave shook his head after them, and retired to his tent.

Inside, he examined his map.

Not far, not far, he thought as he studied the map. More than half the way had been covered; today had been a good trek. He was putting the map away when something caught his eye. Across the map, straight as a pair of railroad tracks, were two unbroken mountain ranges. They led from Soviet Turkestan to the mouth of the Lao-Chatze.

If the valley between them was anything like the map, it was a broad highway to and from Asiatic Russia.

Lying on his back, Dave cast around in his memory.

There was such a way, it was well known. Fifty years ago, Kipling had written a book about the danger of Russian invasion of India through Thibet. It had been a constant bogy to the man from India.

But nowadays, the thing seemed remote. Russia was planning no invasion. Of all the countries of Europe and Asia, the U.S.S.R. desired war the least. They had even sold the Chinese railroad to Japan to keep international peace.

And, anyway, these people were not coming from Russia; they were going towards it. Sneaking towards it, in fact. So—

But they were not White Russians, as they said, because they called each other "comrade." And certainly not Communists, or they wouldn't have to sneak towards their own country.

In Dave's trade you had to know your international politics. He blew out the lamp, and worried the problem, until it came clear as a chess board. Trotskyites. Fourth Internationalista. The people Stalin had kicked out of the Soviet. The old line Bolsheviks who were still fighting, under cover, for the world Revolution. Stalin had executed some only recently. France had kicked a bunch of them out.

Dave took a firm grip on the revolver under his pillow and went to sleep.

TWO HOURS LATER he rolled over on his cot, shoved the gun into the dark, and said: "If you move, pal, I'm goin' to blow your ribs out."

There was no noise in the tent but that of two people breathing—himself and another. "Light the lamp, pal," Dave said. "There are matches right next to it."

He kept the gun pressed into these ribs till the light went on. It was the girl.

The disordered contents of the *kilta* that stood in front of her were mute testimony to the activity in which she had been caught. She stammered: "I was just—"

"Looking for a cigarette," Dave said. "I know. They're on the box there, next to the lamp and the matches." His other hand came out from under the covers, patted her back. There was no gun. "Take one," he said. "Sit down. I was bored, anyway, pal. I hate sleeping."

The girl sat on the edge of the bed. Her dark eyes were white-rimmed, there was a dangerous flush under the pallor of her skin; her hand shook as she lit the cigarette.

Dave took one himself, lit it from the girl's, while the other hand still held the gun. He did not let it go; he had no doubt as to the danger of his opponent. "Looking for my papers?" he asked, lightly. "You should have brought a light with you."

"I—I thought I could feel them." She could not meet his eyes.

He snorted. "Your nature is too suspicious. I'm just what I said I was." He reached inside his pillow, took out an oilskin wrapped package, and handed it to her. "Look 'em over, baby."

"No!"

She disdained to touch them. "Of course these are not the right ones." Her cigarette was half-burned away, where Dave's was hardly started.

"What a suspicious nature you have got, babe... I suppose it's the life you lead."

She was on her feet instantly, her eyes blazing. "What do you know about my life?... Who sent you to watch us?"

"Santa Claus, pal. I'm just a side show man."

"I warn you," she cried, "if I shout, Max and Fernand will kill you. They are waiting in our tent."

"If they cross the line between the two camps, my coolies will blow their heads off," Dave lied calmly. "I gave instructions that you could come in here... You've crushed your cigarette. Have another one."

She stamped on the crushed cigarette, stood over the bed looking down at him. For a moment she was striking in her anger, her fear, her intensity. Then she dropped down to sit beside him, and she didn't stop there; she kept on bending till her hands were on his shoulders, her face burrowing into his chest "I—I'm so miserable," she moaned. "I hate this life so. They make me do it. They threatened to kill me." Her face moved on his chest, as though she were crying.

He let her stay there for a good two minutes, but he kept his hold on the gun, his eyes on the tent flap. Then he said: "Pleasant, but not very convincing. You ought to take a course in acting some place; I've been worked on by profess—"

She slid from his loose grasp, and darted out of the tent.

It was then that Dave McNally made his big mistake. He called: "Remember me to Trotsky."

Instantly he was sorry. In the minds of these people who lived in a world of plot and counterplot, that would damn him as a spy. It would never occur to them that anyone could find out their identity accidentally.

He looked under the cot. His gun cases were still safe. He had tied them to the side bar of the cot.

Still holding the revolver under the pillow, Dave McNally knocked off some more sleep.

5

THE VALLEY OF LAO-CHATZE

WHEN HE AWOKE in the morning, and came out of his tent, the other camp had been broken. Henry, the head porter, explained: "Those people big fools, sah. Get up in cold, hustle like devil, go 'long. Only got two portahs, now, sah."

It was a fact. Dave's train had been enlarged to twelve. "Where do they think we're going?" he asked. "We'll pass them on the trail."

"Yes, sah," Henry said. "Maybe so they shoot at us, sah."

"It's always a thought. Scared, 'Enry?"

"Oh, no, sah. You pretty damn' good shot. No thing those fellahs shoot at all."

"I agree with you there." Dave took his breakfast from the cook-porter, and dragged his bedside box out to sit in the sun and eat. It was deer-liver this morning. High eating in the Himalayas, he thought, and instructed Henry to see that the gun porter walked immediately in front of him. Max and Fernand and the girl must have a gun of some sort, and an accidental bullet might hit one of the coolies. If it was the gun coolie, Dave wanted to be in a position to catch the *kilta*.

Instead of wearing his rifle on his shoulder today, he

carried it cradled in his arms, a cartridge pumped into the chamber. He could have kicked himself for that fool remark last night. The Internationalists were almost certain to try and ambush him now, and he might have to kill one of them. In which case his position with the Abbot of Lao-Chatze Lamasery would be dubious, since Red Abbots do not approve of killing. And his position with the British more so, since the Empire is very firm on the subject.

He felt remarkably fine, for all the impending danger. The altitude seemed to agree with him, now that he was used to it; and the caravan went along rapidly, with twelve men to do the work of eight.

They were scarcely out an hour when he bagged a snow leopard; there was a halt while the coolies skinned it, and then another one a few minutes later for a pair of mountain sheep. So it was nearly noon when Henry suddenly came to a point and the coolies dropped.

But this was no cat, no food animal. It was the fat Internationalist, the greasy one, Max. He was lying on a rock far above them, a rifle barrel glinting in front of his hands. The barrel pointed down on the trail, but not at them.

DAVE CALLED SOFTLY: "Henry! Come here." The head porter slid past the prone carriers, and looked at him expectantly.

"What do you think that man's doing up there?" Dave asked.

Henry chuckled. "Fat man plenty fool. He waiting for you to come by. Forgot the trail turns; you get him now, save trouble latah."

"Oh, yeah? Just shoot the old boy in cold blood, eh?"

Dave shook his head. "The British would like that, 'Enry. You want to see me land in the hoose-gow?"

"Do not understand, please, sah."

"I'll get into trouble if I shoot him, I don't want trouble."

"Please, sah, that very bad man. Beats coolies, makes troubles, *Angrezi* no mind."

"The English would mind plenty." Dave chewed his lip. "If we could sneak up on him from the back, and get his rifle—Got a couple of boys could make it up there, Henry? He'd never hear them."

"Please, no, sah. You white man, you shoot him."

That was in line with the old motto of Asia: when the white man fights, the native runs away.

"No soap," Dave said tersely. "Tell the caravan to move along."

"No, sah."

"What?" Dave glared at his head porter. But the man was firm. He would not walk into any ambush. "You know that fat man couldn't hit anything with that gun," Dave said. "Move along, now."

When the porter still stood, Dave slowly raised the rifle. He was going to force the coolies to take him on up the trail; but he thought better of it. They'd only desert him as they had the Russians.

He looked up again. The fat man suddenly looked around, saw him, scrambled to his feet, and disappeared. Dave was a quick thinker; he had to be. Henry was facing him, the other porters were lying on their faces. He threw the rifle up and fired.

Henry turned.

"I got him," Dave said. "He fell right off that rock."

"Yas sah," Henry said. "Gorge plenty deep here, sah. Nobody ever find that fat man again." He shouted to the caravan to move along.

But Dave knew that the trouble was not ended. There would be another ambush. As they went on up the shoulder of the mountain, he studied each rock formation as they came to it, looking for the rifle which might kill....

IN MOST PLACES the mountain over the ledge bulged so that a shot from above was impossible. But each time the leader went around a curve—which was every five minutes—he held his breath. It was not entirely the rare atmosphere that was making his heart pound so.

The sun shone brightly, the air was beginning to warm with the sun—and then a sudden storm. It blew up from the gorge below with all the ferocity that Dave had known these mountains possessed when they turned themselves loose.

The coolies kept going, with rain lashing at them, and a fierce wind nearly tearing them from the ledge. Dave was drenched in a moment. His snowy white helmet melted; he pulled it off and tossed it into the gorge.

The going was terrifyingly slippery underfoot. Twice the rain loosened boulders from overhead, and they came thundering down the mountain. But long before Dave's untrained ears knew about the landslides, the coolies had heard, and were huddling tight against the ledge, and when the stones and dirt and boulders came, they passed in front of them, harmlessly.

"This country," Dave muttered to himself, "is going to be safe from civilization for a long, long time. In fact," he added, as a sheet of water streamed over the trail and then washed away again with a new change of wind, "if I ever get out of here, it's going to be safe from McNally, too." He wanted to call to Henry to stop for a while, but he knew that if he passed a message forward, the head porter would come back to talk to him, and he was in no mood to watch Henry do his trick of passing the carriers on a trail no wider than half a man.

Ten minutes later, the storm stopped, and, with no more warning than it had given when it went, the sun turned on again with a fierceness that instantly made his head ache. It did not take two minutes for the terrain to dry out again.

This time he did call a halt. While he was rummaging in one of the *kiltas* for a new helmet to protect his head from the sun, Henry said, quietly: "You no hit fat man, sah. He back there." He gestured over his shoulder.

"Huh?" Where?" Dave looked up from the *kilta*, genuinely astonished.

"We pass in storm, sah. Him and other two hiding under rock from rain. They no see us, sah, but 'Enry, he see them."

"O.K." Dave found a helmet, shoved it on. "Let's go. It's just as well I didn't kill the mugg. They'll never catch us, now."

"No, sah," the boss coolie smiled. "They no have portahs, now."

Dave's mouth fell open as he counted. Sometime during the storm, when McNally had been slogging along with his head down, the last two of the Russians' carriers had joined Dave's train. There were fourteen *kiltas* in the line now.

"And I call myself an observant man," Dave marvelled. He wondered what the Russians had done now. And it occurred to him that the coolies understood a lot more of what was going on than he suspected. They had spotted the other gang as troublemakers, and they didn't want any part of it.

They ate lunch, marched some more, shot game, camped that night, and ate another lunch without seeing or hearing from the Russians. And then the ledge suddenly split; there was one path going downhill, winding away through the constant mist, and one going up hill. According to his map, the downhill path led to the Valley of Lao-Chatze....

HE CALLED HENRY again. "Down there," he said. He pointed.

"No game there, sah. We go up this way."

"T'ell with that. I'm paying for this party, Henry; I want to go down the hill."

Henry looked at him placidly. "Shooting not allowed in theah, sah. That is very holy valley, belongs to lamas."

"I know it." This was the time for the showdown. "I want to pay a short visit to the Abbot of Lao-Chatze. All I want of you is to take me to the mouth of the valley and wait for me there. You don't have to go in."

Henry said: "No understand, sah."

"Yeah?" Dave grinned. "You understand what you want to, pal. Half your gang have deserted that other party; I'm willing to lay mandarins to monkeys they expect me to alibi them with the boss when we get back. In fact, pal, I wouldn't be surprised if they had agreed to pay you a little for influencing me."

Henry suddenly smiled one of his rare grins. "McNally *Sahib* is a very wise *Sahib*," he said, in perfect imitation of a British officer's Indian servant. "But please, sah, you give us writing we warned you not to enter valley. In case you do not come back."

"O, K.," Dave said. He looked long and levelly at Henry. "And, Henry—if you think that writing will let you go back before I come out of the valley—you are a lot dumber than I think you are, Henry."

Henry bowed again. "O.K., sah," he said. He turned and shouted at the coolies. He was evidently a man to be respected; the line went down hill without a demur.

Dave McNally felt pretty good. This had been an easy expedition as expeditions went; and here he was at the mouth of the Valley that was his destination.

6

THE GIANT ABBOT

DAVE MCNALLY WENT on alone the next morning. He carried a staff, and nothing more; the instinct that was his stock in trade told him this was no time to be armed. When he reached the first turn in the trail, he looked back; Henry and the other coolies were staring after him sadly. He waved, and went around the corner.

The trail led down grade at a terrific rate. The calves of his legs ached with the strain of holding back; he had a terrifying feeling that he was about to lose control and get going so fast that he would be carried over one of the sharp turns in the ledge, and dashed to the bottomless pits below.

For they did seem bottomless; looking over the edge he saw nothing but mist that seemed as thick as water.

Each hundred feet carried him ten feet nearer that vaporous ocean; and when the time came for lunch, the first tendrils of it were reaching across the edge of the trail.

He squatted with his back against the cliff and ate the lunch he had carried in his pocket, canned beef and biscuits and a flask of water. Then he pressed on, hurriedly, not liking the feeling of loneliness at all.

In a half an hour he was in the middle of the clouds. Dank, cold terror filled him; there was no seeing the trail, no knowing where he was going. He tried to check his breakneck speed, but it was hard to keep from hurrying.

His staff tapped ahead of him, and twice went over the edge and hit nothing at all, while Dave McNally pressed back, standing still, hugging the sweet roughness of the cliff with his heart beating wildly.

His whole brain, his whole body cried: Turn back, turn back. Go back to Henry, let him take you back to the silly Englishman at Durok and his friend Smithers. Go back where there is sunlight and people talking, and English clubs.

You can stop in Malay, the drumming of his heart said, and go on an animal hunt. You'll make your expenses that way, the trip won't be wasted.

Don't go on through a world without light on a slippery ledge over nothing to meet an eight foot Thibetan monk who reads the future. There's no such person, it is *Maya*, illusion, he is just a figment of this world where nothing lives and everything is fog, fog, fog.

IT WAS THEN that something came flapping up out of the infernal depths, and, crying wildly, flew within a foot of Dave's face. The American smelt a horrible smell, as of death itself, and he threw up his arms and knew this was the end.

The creature flapped off in alarm, and mad, hysterical laughter seized the American. It had been a buzzard, the bird of death, coming up from dining on carrion at the foot of the gorge.

The laughter would not stop. Dave flung himself down on his face on the rock, beat at the trail till his hands bled;

and finally he fought for and got control of himself again. He rolled over on his back and lay there gasping.

Then, slowly, he rolled to his knees, got on his feet and found his staff. He was going on, down into the valley. It was true that he could turn back without any great financial loss; but he had never turned back from an expedition before. And if he did not go on, all his life he would know that once he had been yellow; and all his life he would wonder if, once, he had not been near the greatest theatrical attraction of his career, and turned back before he reached it.

He went on, as slowly as he could; the clouds made the rocks slippery as glass.

As he went, he sang at the top of his voice. And what he sang were the most banal and obvious Tin Pan Alley songs he could think of; the kind that shrill singers moaned in the cheap night clubs off Times Square. It made home seem nearer.

At five in the afternoon he knew he was not going to make it. Henry had said that it was only a day's walk. Dave had wasted too much time feeling his way along, and he had not the vaguest idea how long he had spent having hysterics.

Night was going to fall before he reached the monastery. Night on a Himalaya ledge, without fire, without bedding.

He stopped, took some quinine, washed it down with a little water from his flask, and slowly consumed a bar of hard chocolate. Afterwards he forced himself to rest ten minutes, though his body craved action; then he got up and went along, looking for a place on the ledge wide enough to make a safe sleeping place.

THE WHITE CLOUDS were already turning gray when he thought he saw an opening in the cliff that might be a ledge. He poked at it with his staff, and the staff went in. He knelt, and was still a moment, then he thought he heard soft footsteps behind him. He pulled himself back from the cave, but not in time.

Strong hands seized him, lifted him off his feet. Dave McNally shouted, though there was no one to hear; he kicked out backwards. But whoever held him must be tremendously strong; he couldn't struggle free. His hands were firmly, almost gently, pulled behind his back, for all his struggles; soft ropes looped his wrists and tied them.

They caught his ankles the same way, as a blacksmith ties a kicking horse; then set him down. Through the fog he caught a glimpse of two of the tallest men he had ever seen; Thibetans, each nearly seven feet tall, their saffron faces, calmly grim.

One of them picked him up and tossed him over his shoulder; then they started down the trail at a breakneck pace.

There was no use in looking where they were taking him; the world was all fog, and soon it was all black fog. Gradually Dave relaxed, and then he was conscious of a queer thing; strength was flowing out of the man who was carrying him.

This strength was a tangible thing, as water, as ink. Dave felt it bathe his relaxed body with soft, strong caresses, like luke warm water; gradually, from merely being prone, he felt the muscles, first of his legs, then of his body, finally of his neck and arms, go as lax as death.

It became pleasant to be carried along, and from merely

pleasant it became ecstatic, a wonderful heady feeling. There was no reason why a man shouldn't sleep; he would not be harmed. No reason why a man—

When Dave awoke, the sun was shining, and he felt better than he could ever remember feeling before. He sat up and looked around him.

He was in a courtyard, lying on a pallet of straw. In the center of the courtyard was a space of dirt, in which flowers grew and a fountain played; around this were flaggings of many different colors. His pallet had been placed on the flaggings.

He got up, a little surprised that he was no longer tied. His clothing had been taken away, and he was dressed in a long yellow robe, like a kimono. Under this he wore his own underclothing, but they had been washed and ironed; and next to his skin—and this was the greatest surprise of all—was his money belt.

He got it out, opened it. Its contents were intact. The gold he had brought; the pictures of New York, his American passport. He went and washed his face and hands, and strolled around the courtyard, looking for an exit, and, at the same time, examining a series of statues set in niches around the wall. There was lettering under them, but he was not enough of an Orientalist to tell whether it was Chinese, Thibetan, or even Japanese. But he recognized the images: there was Buddha, fat and contemplative, Siva, the Hindu Bullgod, Mohammed, sleek and rather commercial—this was no image he had ever seen, but recognizable from portraits—the Krishna who brings sons to Indian mothers, the many-breasted goddess of the Burmese, and more. There were all the gods and prophets of the Orient represented there.

He found the gate, too, but steel bars were padlocked across it. The padlock was a thing of beauty, lined and engraved with strange figures. He was holding it in his hand and examining it when he heard the voice behind him, deep as the bellow of Siva, soft as the dove who was one of the Buddhist signs of deception.

He turned, and then for a moment, Dave McNally, slick American showman, brave and tough leader of expeditions, was speechless.

The man who confronted him was tall. There were eight feet of him, but he was no giant as Dave knew the phrase. This man bore none of the stigmata of glandular disorder that mark the circus freak. For this man was perfectly proportioned, though a little heavy. He was dressed in a saffron robe similar to Dave's; but his was figured with faint gold thread designs, mystic, but almost erased by wear.

On his head was the huge red tam o'shanter that marks the lamas of Thibet!

7

THE MAGIC MAN

DAVE FELT HIS spine bending despite himself. After a moment, he bowed. Then he jerked himself upright again, annoyed because this man had smiled. This was not the way he had planned it. He had intended to barge in here, proposition the Abbot, flatter him with lies about America's interest in Thibetan religion, wave some money under his nose, and get him onto a ship. He had intended to bring an interpreter.

The Abbot said, in very English English: "Mr. McNally, isn't it? You are a music hall man, aren't you, Mr. McNally.... Oh, yes, I speak English because I was educated at Oxford...."

Dave thought: "The old boy went through my papers." He gained confidence with the thought.

"Yes, I looked over the papers in your belt, Mr. McNally. Quite so."

Fear was creeping into Dave's heart, and it was something akin to the fear he had felt on the trail. This man knew too much; it was like being naked before bayonets. He tried to bluff it out; hell, it was an act. "O.K., pal. I heard you were a mystic."

The Abbot smiled, and looked down from his great

height. "You mustn't try to bluff me, McNally. After all, I'm so much bigger than you, y'know, and I'm home. And, please, don't be afraid of me. Our cult doesn't care for bloodshed."

Dave said: "I'm glad you speak English. Your cult?" He waved his hand around the walls. "You've got every god in Asia here. D'ya worship 'em all?"

"Your effort to be—you Americans call it tough?— tough, is credible. No, we don't worship these men. Though each taught us something. We are beyond that. All gods are illusion, except the god that dwells within each man; the god of perfection. To bring the human mind to its fruition; where nothing is wasted, where each thought is used, where no secret can be concealed—that is godhood. We seek it, though we doubt if we shall ever attain it, but in the seeking we hope to attain merit." His voice dropped down to the Buddhist soliloquy, the appeal to the Buddha who was also Guatama the teacher: *"Om padne ame—"*

Then the tall lama shook his head, and said: "Pardon me. There is kindness to one's fellow selves, too, all humans, bound on the wheel of desire. There are two new Asiatic gods we do not exhibit, yet, Mr. McNally—the statues are being prepared. Come with me."

HE LED THE dazed McNally to a panel of soapstone intricately carved in bas-relief. "Beautiful, isn't it?" he admitted absently. "There was a time when the great Chinese merchants worshipped it—that is, they worshipped the beautiful in workmanship, to the exclusion of everything else." The stone panel swung in, and the Abbot led the way through. A servant or lay brother swung the panel behind them. They went down a long, cool corridor; the monk rapped at the solid wall and it opened.

He explained: "That is one of the steps of the novitiate: to make a piece of craft so fine that it defies detection. Thus we teach the principle of patience."

Within the cell was a man, working with a tiny chisel and mallet on a full-relief statue. The work was nearly done; it seemed to be springing from the solid rock. McNally looked, and then was entranced.

The figure was that of a man, a working man. One brawny arm was holding up a hammer; his legs had corded muscles in them. This at first glance; then it became apparent that the strong man was, as the Abbot would say, illusion; it was the statue, actually, of a man who had never had strength, a puny man, who yet looked in the mirror and saw himself powerful.

The Abbot read Dave's mind softly: "You are quick to perceive, Mr. McNally. That is right—it is the god of the Siberian intellectuals, of Lenin who knew he was weak and ailing, but saw himself as the personification of the man who worked with his strong back. It is, Mr. McNally, Communism."

Dave gritted his teeth. This was no act; this giant in the saffron robe really read minds. He would not think, he told himself, he would stop thinking; to think was to lay yourself open to the Abbot, and to be absorbed, destroyed.

The Abbot said gently to the workman, who had never looked up: "You do well, Graves. Persevere."

The workman said, in English: "Yes, master."

Dave was caught off guard again. For the workman was an Englishman. But, like everyone else he had seen at the monastery, he seemed tremendously tall; taller than the guards who had brought him in, nearly as tall as the Abbot's eight feet.

THE ABBOT CAUGHT Dave's arm and led him out. "Yes," he said, "it is no use trying to stop thinking. You have not yet got power over your mind. You are right, Graves was an Englishman. A captain in the army in India. He came here out of curiosity; he remained to apply for a novitiate. He will be a monk in another ten years."

Dave said nothing. He concentrated on that word: nothing, nothing, nothing.

"His height?" The Abbot asked. "Of course, each acolyte must grow; we thus teach them to control their own bodies. You have seen Hindus and Yogis who can stop their blood from circulating, who stick knives into themselves and do not breathe? They are on the right path, but always there is the distraction of the world, greed, vanity, lust. When you have surpassed these, Mr. McNally, you can make yourself grow, change the color of your hair, control your body in every respect. Now shall we see the other new god, the—"

"No!" McNally's voice came from his lips in a croaking groan. "No more."

The Abbot said scornfully; "Your fear is only illusion. You will overcome it."

Dave turned, and the tall man was gone. The American staggered down the corridor in the direction of the court-yard. The servant, not looking at him, opened the soap-stone panel, and Dave went through into the sunshine. It was then he remembered that there should be no sunshine there; that this monastery should be under the blanket of eternal fog that filled the valleys.

Exhausted, terrified as he had never been frightened by any physical danger, he went over to his straw pallet, and flung himself down.

HE WOKE UP after a while, grinned, and rolled over on his back on the straw pallet to stare at the sun. His cigarettes were on a little table near his hand; he lit one, and there was all the fragrance of New York in it.

Wasn't he a tough guy, the toughest in one of the most dangerous jobs in the world? The men who collected soldiers could use guns; the sideshow considered soldiers sissies because the man had to use diplomacy. There is nothing harder in the world than carrying a gun and not using it when your life is threatened.

He had done that, standing under other men's guns. He had gone up against the Brazilian pygmies who blow poisoned darts at strangers, and he had talked to them in sign language—not knowing a syllable of their elemental tongue—and persuaded them first to lay down their blow pipes with their tiny messengers of instant death, and then, finally, to come to the United States with him.

That adventure had ended up by his teaching the pygmy chief poker, on the boat.

He, Dave McNally, was tough, tough. He had spent his life where no one else cared to go; and he had usually come back with the goods. The six continents and the seven seas knew him, and they knew him as a man of peace, who could walk among destruction and warfare and sudden death and not be afraid.

Pygmies or giants, it was all one to him, and as for mindreaders, they were starving to death in every cheap rooming house off Times Square.

He had come too soon from the jungle to the mountains, and he was a little liverish, as the English would say. That was why the big Abbot had bluffed him before. But he was still McNally.

Holding the cigarette between his fingers, he rose and went to the soapstone panel. He knocked on it, and said, clearly: "I want to see the boss of this joint again. And I want my clothes." He was above trying to talk in any language but his own. They'd understand.

He turned from the panel, puffing on the cigarette, and just caught himself in time to keep from blinking. The Abbot was standing across the courtyard, smiling at him placidly. "Your clothes are being cleaned, Mr. McNally. They are in good hands."

"Nice of you," Dave said quietly. "You put out a fine brand of hospitality here. Have a cigarette?"

"No, thanks, I don't smoke. But you said you wanted to see me."

Dave kept away from the Abbot. If he stood too close he would have to cock his head back, to talk, and that was undesirable. "Why, yes, I did. I suppose you've been wondering what I was doing here? I remember, you said you knew I was in show business."

"No, Mr. McNally, I haven't been wondering."

It was necessary to keep on looking the Abbot straight in the eye, but it was also difficult. "Well, here's the set-up, Abbot. Your fame has reached America; people there have heard about you. I'm here to see about getting you to go back to the United States with me on a lecture tour."

The Abbot smiled. "Your courage does you credit. Do I look like a music hall attraction?"

Dave laughed. "There's more to show business than that." He was getting along O.K. "We would route you through the university towns, get you to address the classes in philosophy, arrange meetings with the greatest minds of our country."

"Under the management of Jake Loeb? Like the gorilla you brought him?"

"How did you—"

"It was in your mind, Mr. McNally. Really, if I didn't admire your courage I might feel insulted. You wouldn't want that, would you, Mr. McNally?" The voice was suave.

"No," Dave said quickly. "Because you're my host. But now, Abbot, listen. Don't you want to spread your cult? You owe it to the world to tell people about—" He stopped. Inside his head there was a roaring and an emptiness like that in a Himalayan gorge. He staggered over to his pallet, and went down on his knees. "Touch of fever—" he muttered. He didn't believe it.

"Finish your speech, Mr. McNally," the lama said gently. "Why don't you go on?" His voice came from a great distance away. Dave McNally wondered what it was he had been going to say, and then he—didn't—wonder—any—more—

8

ESCAPE

WHEN HE AWOKE, he knew at once that he was not alone. It was still shining in the courtyard; but whether he had slept an hour or twenty-four he could not say. He looked around; now there were four pallets including his own.

The three Trotsky people had been captured, too.

He crept over and shook the girl's shoulder; not because he was very glad to see her, but because she spoke English. She muttered in her sleep.

He carried water from the fountain and splashed it in her face. That brought her to, but drowsily. She said something in Russian, then recognized him. "Nice work, comrade. What are you going to do to us."

"I'm a prisoner, too. This is the Monastery of Lao-Cha-tze."

"Yeah, I remember. Two big muggs jumped us on the trail, and picked up Fernie and Max. I—I walked along. I didn't want to, but—how long have we been here?"

"I don't know. I keep going off into trances. It's—say, what were you people doing on the trail down to here? This isn't the way to Russia."

She looked at him. "Fernie was right then. You were on to us. Only we weren't going to Russia. We were coming here. Fernand is half-Chinese; he said that the Abbot here had more influence than any man in the Orient. We were going to ask him to help us."

Dave McNally laughed bitterly. "You had a swell hunch there, pal. He'll tell you that revolution is only illusion." He dropped down on the pallet next to her. "We've got to get out of here. He'll turn us all into monks."

"He'd have a hard time with me."

Dave said: "He could change your sex if he wanted to. He could do anything. He makes his students grow a couple of feet just to prove to them that the mind is stronger than the body."

"You sound a little frightened, comrade. Tell me, who were you working for—the British or the Soviets? Max said—"

Dave told her: "Neither. I was working for myself. The story I told you happened to be true. I heard about this mind-reading priest who was eight feet tall, and I came up here to persuade him to go back to the United States with me and make a few vaudeville dates." He laughed, scornfully. "I thought the thing was a master fake of some sort."

"And—"

"It isn't, sister. Not yet, anyhow!"

She said: "Look—" The monosyllable was on a rising inflection, long drawn out, the last sound was almost a scream.

"That's the boss," Dave said. "The Abbot himself. It's magic, sister. It must be. But I can't figure it!"

THE HUGE MAN came across the courtyard to them. As he came, moving lightly, his feet invisible under the long robe, Max and Fernand sat up slowly on their pallets. The

Abbot spoke to each of them in a language Dave did not understand. He whispered to the girl: "What's he saying?"

"Nothing much," she whispered back, "he told Max in Russian that he was quite safe, not to worry. He was speaking Chinese or something to Fernie."

The Abbot could not possibly have heard them. But he turned his finely shaped head slowly, and said: "I just made them welcome to the Monastery, Mr. McNally. If you will come with me, now, I will give you dinner for the three of you. You see, no one but I may talk to an outsider; only the Abbot is considered above distraction." He walked slowly away.

The girl said harshly: "Hey, I'm here." She spat something in Russian. The Abbot did not turn.

Dave dropped a hand on her shoulder. "Probably part of his religion. Not even the Abbot can talk to a woman. Y'know, it makes me feel better. The guy's human after all."

He and Max followed the Abbot to a panel of sandstone that opened to disclose a tray set with three services and a large bowl of food. Max took one end, Dave the other; they carried it back.

"You can eat out of my plate, pal," Dave said, as the two revolutionaries fell to without worrying about the girl. "By the way," he added, with his mouth full, "what's your name?"

"Rita. Say this is good food. The only decent meal we've had in Thibet except the chow you stood us on the trail."

Dave said: "When the revolution gets here, you'll eat quail every day and like it. Y'know, I feel better. In fact I feel pretty hot. Ever since I saw that the old boy was afraid of you—"

She said: "I wonder what this is we're eating?... What do you expect me to do? Vamp the old boy? He won't even look at me."

"Hardly that," Dave said, "but at least I can think about how he's scared of you when he starts giving me the mystic act."

He felt almost brash. There was still a chance that the Abbot might listen to his proposition. And if not—

They put down the empty plate, and still he felt good. And then—the soapstone screen opened, and the Abbot appeared. "A pleasant meal?" he asked. All four of them answered that it had been. Max said: "A curry of lamb, wasn't it? Quite—"

Horror stricken, Dave realized that Max was talking in Russian and that he could understand him. He looked at the Abbot. The tall man seemed to be saying: "Tomorrow you enter the novitiate. It takes twenty years—" but his lips weren't moving.

Dave concentrated hard on this: he's nothing but a phony mindreader. I've seen 'em before. He's scared of dames, he doesn't dare even look at this Rita. He's scared—

Dave found he could no longer hear the Abbot talk. When he looked around the tall man's lips were not moving; perhaps they never had moved. The head of the Lamasery went away again, as noiselessly as he had come.

Max said something, but Dave could not understand it. He wiped a sweating brow with the sleeve of his gown. He whispered to the girl: "We have to get out of here—tonight."

"Not till Fernand gets an answer from the Abbot. That's what we came here for."

Dave said: "Look at Fernand. Look at Max." His voice was contemptuous.

She looked. The two men were rapt, their eyes raised to the sky; they did not know they were not alone. The girl spat something at them in one of her many languages; neither heard. Max got up after a moment, and walked, like a somnambulist, to an Ikon set in the wall; the old sign of the Russian Orthodox Church. He knelt and began to pray.

"Max," the girl cried in English. "They were our enemies. We swore to destroy—" She stopped when she saw they were not listening to her.

In the silence that followed, Fernand said, slowly: "*Om mane, padne hum, Om mane padne hum.*"

THE GIRL SAID brokenly: "We came here to make a convert. We lost two of the best—"

"I'll get you back to Durok," Dave said. "After that, it's up to you."

They sat there, side by side. Max was still praying, pouring his heart out to the Ikon; Fernand was sitting in the cross-legged Buddhistic attitude, mumbling to himself, and counting the beads of a non-existent prayer necklace.

Suddenly there was someone else in the courtyard. Dave braced himself for another encounter with the Abbot; but it was a servant come to take away the dishes. When his bowed face came near to Dave's, the American saw, with a shock, that it was Graves, the Englishman who had been working on the idol that was to represent Communism.

"Graves," Dave hissed. "Do you want to get out of here?" The Englishman did not answer; there was an Oriental repose in his features.

" 'Ten-*shun!*" Dave barked, suddenly. His voice was low, intense.

The Englishman dropped the tray, his powerful shoulders, under the saffron robe straightened. His face relaxed, he said, weakly: "I thought—I—was—"

He faltered.

"Hold it, Graves," Dave said. "You've been hypnotized. Do you get it? Yogi, or something like that. You're in a Lamasery, and you want to get out."

"Not—any—more," Graves said. "I—don't want to leave."

"Who told you that?" Dave asked. He was working fast; Graves was slipping back. "Who told you that?"

"He did," Graves said. "The Master. I must go. I should not talk, I am—"

"Stop it!" Dave asked, insistently: "What regiment do you belong to?"

"Fifteenth Lahore Cavalry—who are you?" The last question was sharp and crisp as any British officer of troopers.

"I've come to get you," Dave said. "We're leaving, getting out. Now. You know the way. Take us, Graves!"

The captain said: "All right. You should have said so." He swung energetically across the courtyard. Dave grabbed the girl's hand and followed.

A DOOR OPENED at Graves' approach. When they went through there was a lay servant bowing to them; evidently Graves had gained some standing in the monastery. They passed out, and then they were in a rubbly field, stumbling over rocks.

Dave said: "This is too easy. If they come after us, Rita,

it's up to you to stop them. I think they're not allowed to touch a woman."

"I—I'll try."

The edge of the field was the end of the world. It stopped abruptly. Below was nothing but fog. Dave McNally understood then why there had been sunshine in the monastery; it was built on a plateau rising from some narrow peak inside a gorge.

Graves stopped, puzzled. Dave wandered the edge, quartering it like a bird dog; he found a way down that they could use by swinging down from one bush to the next.

Graves stopped, and said, abruptly: "He calls. I must—" He turned back.

Dave shouted: "No, go on!" Then he turned. There were footsteps behind him, stumbling over the rubble.

His fingers seemed to be all thumbs as they fumbled with the buckle of his money belt. He did not get it off till the first monastery servant was towering over him; then he swung.

The lay brother had been swinging with a long iron rod; he stopped abruptly and went down like a poled ox when the gold pouch of the belt landed on his head.

There was another man; Dave swung at him, but the servant warded the blow with his rod, and it slid along. Huge hands grasped for Dave; he shouted: "Rita!" and the man let go as the girl's small hand went out for him.

Dave swung again while the servant was trying to protect himself from the contaminating touch of the woman; this swing ended in a knock out blow.

Graves was still standing on the edge of the precipice; his face was dreamy, enchanted. Dave grabbed the girl, said: "Kiss him. It may break the charm—" and thrust her at the Britisher.

She was quick to get the idea; she had to reach high to get her arms around his neck, pull his massive head down. With the touch of her lips, the spell broke again, and Captain Graves said, thickly: "Helen!"

Dave started down the path, sliding to a bush, catching at it, hauling the girl in once when she almost slid past him. The next half hour was chaos, mad chaos as they nearly slid to their death not once but a dozen times. They were in the fog now, and Dave could only tell that the others were still near him by the noise of the gravel under their feet, by the occasional contact of their bodies as they ran into each other.

Graves stopped them suddenly on a little thank-you-ma'am. "We are nearly at the bottom," he said. "They keep two guards posted there. I was one of them myself, long ago."

"We'll have to land on them from above," Dave said. "I wish I could see."

"Let me go first," Captain Graves suggested. "I'll lead them under you. I think—I'm sure—the bottom's only a drop below us."

"O.K., Captain." Dave heard the big man go off, shouting in Thibetan. This was the worst, this waiting. Nothing happened then for a long time, or what seemed long; and then there were voices directly below.

DAVE GOT A firm grip on the money belt and dropped. Through the fog the descent seemed endless; then he landed on something soft and rolling. It might be Graves but he couldn't be sure; he swung the belt, and the man dropped, Dave still sprawling across his shoulders.

Graves shouted: "Here, old man, here. I'm holding him." But before Dave could locate him, the girl came down from above, and he heard a thud.

"A rock'll do," she said. "That one did. Let's go."

They found the rock ledge, and started up it. Up and up and up through the fog; but the fog and the rocks and the narrow trail held no terrors for Dave McNally now. He had seen worse.

Sometime that morning, the fog lifted for a moment. The girl stopped them with a shriek. "He—he got us, too," she said. "McNally. You're as big as—as he is. And I'm only a little smaller. I—he be—"

Graves said: "No. I—I've shrunk again. I—well I didn't want to mention it. I feel smaller."

"Smaller hell!" said McNally. "You never were large. It was only an illusion. See—your clothes still fit!"

The girl said: "I'm going to stop. I feel funny."

They crouched against the ledge. They were still crouching there when they heard voices. McNally said, sharply: "They've come after us." He unbuckled the belt again, crouched on the path.

"No," Graves said. "No. They're English voices. English!"

Through the fog they came, the Resident, and another man in hunting clothes. The Resident cried: McNally. You're safe. I—your porter, that Henry chap sent a runner back. He said you'd been gone a week, and could he come home?"

"A week?" Dave shook his head. "I didn't know it was a day."

The Resident said: "This is Mr. Nabors, of the Mission Board. He—"

Graves said: "A Minister? I—I think I'd like to talk to you. I've been living with the devil."

Everything was getting normal again. There was Henry, and the other porters. "I say," the Resident said. "This will make quite a story to tell back home in America. Won't it, now."

"I'll never mention it," Dave said devoutly. "They'd laugh me out of the country!" He sighed. "But, I'll figure these magic-men out yet or die trying!"

9

TRICKS OF THE TRADE

DAVE SAW THE girl again. Three months later. He was sitting in the cocktail lounge of the Raffles Hotel in Singapore when she came in with two other men. Dave had had good hunting on the Malayan peninsula. Down in the harbor, he had a load of menagerie animals all ready for shipment.

The girl hadn't changed much, but she looked healthier and a little sleek. She was well-dressed and it was apparent that she was with two educated and cultured men.

Dave jumped up and went over.

"Rita," he said. "Hello, sister! I never expected—"

Rita turned and stared at him. There was no recognition in her somber eyes. She looked through him. Politely, she said, "I'm afraid you've made a mistake. I don't seem to recall having met you before—"

Dave grinned. "Sure. Maybe I look a little different. But I'm McNally. You know. Dave McNally."

"I *know* you've made a mistake now," Rita replied indulgently. She smiled sweetly, then pushed past him to join her two companions who were standing by, waiting for her patiently, but with some quizzical wonder.

They sat down across the room.

Dave sighed and watched her go. She'd put the Indian sign on him. Oh well, he shrugged, what the hell. He returned to his own table and took up his Scotch and soda again.

Five minutes later, a waiter brought him a note.

It read: "Don't try and talk to me. I'm on a dangerous mission. The English police may be watching. Thanks for everything you did and give my regards to old Manhattan."

It was signed, "R." There was a postscript. "We never heard from Max or Fernie again. I've thought and thought and finally decided that the whole thing was just mass hypnotism. Haven't you?"

Dave looked across at her where she sat with the two men, and he slowly shook his head. Then he laughed.

It was too bad he couldn't have talked with her. He wanted to explain—tell her how he had finally fathomed the secrets of the Abbot of Lao-Chatze. Tricks of the trade, that's what they were, as old to Broadway and the main stem as the travelling Hebrew act was to vaudeville.

He could have told her that the Abbot was one of those lucky guys who are versed in telepathy—really versed in the subject. The Abbot had been naturally endowed with telepathic powers. He *was* really able to read minds… But what the hell—so was the Great McCoy who'd been a knockout in the legit and was now pulling down two grand a week in Hollywood.

He could have told her that the Abbot was a hypnotist—could make men believe things which weren't so, could make illusions seem like truths—could make McNally hear a man talking Russian when no one was talking at all—could make Graves think he had grown taller when he hadn't added an inch to his stature.

And the magic men themselves? What would he have told Rita about them?

NOTHING. BECAUSE THEY weren't magic men. None but the Abbot ever showed any sign of magic. Only the Abbot could hypnotize. Only the Abbot could mind-read.

But their height! Rita would have asked Dave about the height of those men in the Valley of Lao-Chatze.

That was a laugh!

There were many explanations.

The one Dave believed in was right down to earth. If a guy like the Abbot wanted to build up a magic-men scene, with himself as the big boss, it would have been pretty simple to keep dosing his clan with shots of pituitary extract. Over a period of time, they would have gotten colossal!

Pituitary extract makes a man big, makes him grow, makes his skin get heavy and coarse, adds weight and height and breadth.

"Sure," Dave thought, "that's what the Abbot did. When you come right down to it, he'd have made a marvelous showman. He had a flair! But maybe it's just as well I missed bringing him back alive. Jake Loeb's got more mindreaders now than he can book."

So he finished his Scotch and soda, rose with his chit, and his eyes bade the glamorous Rita a mute farewell as he left.

THE ISLE OF YELLOW GIRLS

*An Hawaiian Eagle Scout and a Broadway
Frank Buck sail the South Seas to an island
of intrigue and sirens like machines*

1

DAVE MCNALLY LAY on the deck of the *President*, just under the shadow of the cargo boom. The ship was rolling gently, just enough so he could—on a good roll—see a touch of horizon without moving off his back. The sun came down and baked him, and he felt good.

A Kanaka deck hand had been unnecessarily polishing shining brass near him for fifteen minutes. The man, Mac knew, wanted to talk to him; but let it come, let it come. His last expedition had been to the Aleutian Islands after a cargo of bears and seals, and he had had his marrow-full of cold; the Pacific sun made him feel fine, he could tell it was reaching right through him. He had no intention of moving or raising his voice, or doing any other of the silly things more active passengers did.

Finally the Kanaka said, in slightly guttural English: "You are Mr. McNally, sir?"

"That's right," Mac said. He opened his eyes under his sun-goggles, looked at the brawny islander, smiled, and closed his eyes again.

"My brother, Frank, sailed with you some years ago," the Kanaka said. "About ten years ago."

"Yeah?" Mac thought back. "That wasn't a bad trip for those days—I was assembling an orchestra and some hula

dancers for a chain of theaters. Yeah, I remember. Your last name is Panaki, isn't it?"

"Yes, sir!" The Kanaka was pleased. "My name is Tom. Frank has a shop now, back in Hawaii; it is too bad, sir, you did not know; you could have visited him and honored his household."

"You boarded the ship at Hawaii, Tom?" Mac didn't mind talking as long as he didn't have to move. "I didn't notice you on the way out from the mainland."

"Yes, Mr. McNally. I am working my way to the Philippines; last month I was twenty-one, and my father told me to go away and see the world. Frank traveled for a year before he settled down and my middle brother, Larry. Now I go. I have noticed you since we left home, Mr. McNally; always you lie here—not up with the passengers. Are you ill, sir?"

"Naw," the theater man said. "My honored fellow passengers have bad case of Hawaiianitis. They are all busy

LUCIA

learning Hawaiian to use on the way home. Tell me, Tom, what gets into people who visit the Islands? They come away poi-ing and aloha-oeing like they were ashamed of knowing English."

Tom laughed politely. "I do not know, sir. I do not think there are any natives who do not speak English; like my brothers, I am a high school graduate. You go to collect another orchestra?"

Mac said: "No. I've risen above orchestras, Tom. I'm the biggest collector of theatrical novelties in the world; I'll show you the clipping to prove it. Buck gets more animals, but I get human acts too. Now I've got a project on the fire that would make your black hair stand on end, kid; I've heard about the new island they discovered the one that's supposed to have been isolated so long that evolution passed it by. It probably doesn't exist."

"You are right, sir. I saw the story in the newspapers,

but considered it a mere sailor's yarn. But you must have become very wealthy, Mr. McNally, to take such a long trip on such small hope."

"Not I, Tommy. McNally always has an ace in the hole. I'm going to pick up a half-dozen pearl nurses and take 'em for a swimming and diving exhibition; if I can get bathing suits on those Jay girls, they ought to wow 'em on the county-fair circuit."

"I should like to see that, sir. I hear those girls can swim circles around the best Islander."

"Not to mention the fact the swimming-suits—as already mentioned—are strictly tabu. You're through with this ship at Manila, and you're hitting me for a job. Right?"

"You are psychic, Mr. McNally."

"What can you do, Tommy?"

"I took a prize in chemistry at high school, Mr. McNally, and also studied the usual curriculum. I was editor of my school paper, and played on the varsity football team. Also I have some business experience from serving in my brother's shop after school."

"Can you sail a boat, Tom?"

The boy smiled.

"I am a Hawaiian, sir. And I have my Red Cross for first-aid and lifesaving. I was an Eagle Boy Scout and—"

"Whoa, Tommy, whoa! You'll be giving the boss an inferiority complex. You're hired when we get to Manila, get my bags out of stateroom ninety-two and wake me up. I've just come back from Alaska and I'm still a little frozen around the middle. Now go away, and let me sleep."

"Yes, Mr. McNally."

"Oh, and Tommy—"

"Yes, sir?"

"If I catch you even saying so much Hawaiian as 'aloha,' you're fired. Twenty a week okay?"

"Ample, sir, I wish to see the world. And I do not know much Hawaiian, sir."

"Attaboy," Mac said, and went back to sleep.

BY THE TIME they had been in Manila twelve hours, Dave McNally was wondering what he had done all these years without Tom. The boy had found him a three-room suite in a private house; had already hired a seaworthy ketch and an old Filipino to stand watches; and was now buying provisions at about two-thirds the price Mac would have had to pay.

"I must have gone to Sunday school or something when I was a boy," McNally decided. "Now I'm reaping the rewards of a well-spent life." He was dressing in the bedroom of his suite for a call on the editor of one of the local papers. He finished shaving, and, in his shorts, opened the bureau to get out white linens; looking over his shoulder, he saw that Tom had laid out a suit, socks and dark blue silk shirt, with a white tie. McNally's shoes, freshly whitened, sat primly under the edge of the bed.

The showman grinned, and dressed. There must be some awful catch to this Tom Panaki. His brother, while a good sailor, and a nice shot with a rifle, had not been outstanding; McNally had only remembered him because of a special brand of spaghetti sauce he had made one night.

Boy, he thought as he descended to the street and whistled up a two-wheeled pony-taxi—boy, a man was a fool to take those Arctic jobs on. The South Seas for him, every time.

The newspaper editor said, yes, he remembered the piece about the island. Their waterfront man had written it, he'd be in pretty soon. While he was waiting, would Mr. McNally pose for a picture? Distinguished explorer visits Manila, that sort of thing. So Mr. McNally was going to try and find the island mentioned in the story?

"Yeah," Mac drawled. "Make a good side-show attraction. 'The Island Where Time Stood Still.' Might even sell it to a museum; I've got nothing against pure science except the prices it pays."

"That island may not be there," the editor said, "you know these sailor yarns. We really only ran the story to fill space on a Monday; we were quite surprised when the wire services gave it such a play."

Mac said: "This sailor brought back some kind of animal, didn't he?"

The editor laughed. "A rat, I believe—but here's Carran, now, our waterfront man. He can tell you more about it than I can."

Carran said: "Sure, if you want to meet the sailor. That's easy. This foundation bought his rat from him for five hundred bucks, and he used it to make a down payment on a saloon. Come on with me,"

The saloon was named The Biologic Foundation Bar and Grill, in honor of the source of its proprietor's money. This man turned out to be one Pinky Tobias, ex-sailor, copra trader, and general roustabout. He was a little under the weather when Dave arrived.

"Yes, sir, yes, sir—that is quite a place, indeed. Elephant tracks all over the place, and monkeys what could talk like politicians. Parrots with tail feathers that hung on the ground and—"

The reporter looked at Mac, and shrugged. "You're pretty high for this time of day, aren't you, Pinky?"

Pinky blinked. "Who, me? Naw. Well—I had a couple. There was a Kanaka boy in here, eddicated fella, askin' all about the island. 'N, he was so polite, I didn't want to show no race prejudice by refusin' ta drink with him."

"By the name of Tom Panaki?"

"Tom somethin' 'r other."

Mac said, "I might have known. Let me buy you gentlemen a couple of drinks, and then I'll be on my way."

HE STOPPED OFF at the Japanese consulate on his way home, and then at the office of the company that owned the cultivated pearl fisheries. The consulate willingly enough stamped his passport good for visiting the pearl islands and the little Ph.D. at the pearl company said, yes, they could trust Mr. McNally not to steal any of their oysters, but he would have to agree not to talk business to any of the divers who had not served their terms.

"Terms?" Mac asked. "You mean apprenticeship?"

"Precisely, sir," the Japanese said, bowing. "They come to us, you know, when they are nine; we pay their parents a small sum. Then they live on the island, being trained to swim and dive and nurse oysters, until they are fifteen, when they become divers. For the next three years they dive, and then they are released, with a good sum of money for their three years' work. It is a nice arrangement, sir; with the money they are usually the best-dowered girls in their villages."

"Hmm, I see. I suppose the boys are crazy to marry them."

The Japanese giggled. "Not so very as you might suppose, sir. The work is difficult, the life very, very healthy; our girls are a bit on the muscular side."

Mac said: "Even if I didn't need them for an attraction, I'm going to make a point of visiting those islands. Your girls are something no man should miss."

"You will find them very, very interesting, sir."

Mac went back to his rooms and found Tom working on his sea-going clothes. "Well," McNally said, "I went around to the Biologic Bar and Grill, only you'd beat me to it. How about this island?"

"Frankly, Mr. McNally, I believe it's all a lot of tommyrot. Bushwa, as we used to say in high school. This man found a deformed rat, and he has just enough native cunning to build it up into something."

"Was it a rat?"

"It would look like one," said the ex-Eagle Scout. "Actually, it was what is known as a marmosa, a species of— roughly—marsupial rodent. That is, they carry their young in a pouch, as do kangaroos, and opossums. This particular one had some deformity of her mammary system, so that she appeared to sweat milk, as does the duckbilled platypus of Australia."

"Well, people aren't likely to pay much to look at a rat, milk sweating or otherwise. The elephants and parrots and so on are phony, Tom?"

Tom looked up from mending the rope sole of one of McNally's seashoes. "Sit," he said. "By tonight, Pinky will see parrots and elephants in his barroom."

McNally grinned. "Well, I don't know. We might look for cannibals in the Poly—"

"Sir," Tom said, "we might as well try and find this island. I have the position, and it is not far from the cultured pearl preserve; a day's sail."

McNally looked at his helper a little more closely. "You've been looking into those, too, eh?"

The boy met his eyes.

"Sir, since I was a small boy, I have heard about the islands where the girls tend the pearl oysters. My grandfather—he was Japanese—once visited there, and he said it was like eating lotus, sir, if you will pardon an expression from the classics."

McNally frowned. "Kid, don't get smarter than the boss. It makes me uneasy… We sail high tide tonight, then. Tell your crew to be aboard."

"Yes, Mr. McNally." The boy put the shoe down carefully.

2

THE CREW—HIS NAME was Cecil—stood by to fend them off from the pier. Tom had the wheel, and so McNally had appointed himself bow lookout. He could sail well enough himself, but he preferred letting the Hawaiian take them out of Manila harbor.

Their course was southeast, and the Southern Cross lay on the horizon, a group of bright stars widely spaced, no more striking, no more spectacular, than any other stars, but still romantic because of association.

"The Russians gypped us when they sold us Alaska for six million dollars," Dave McNally said. "Or was it a jug of whisky? Anyway, they gypped us, gold and sealskins to the contrary notwithstanding. Hey, Tom!"

"Yes, sir?"

"Let's save our money and buy Alaska to give back to the Russians."

"Yes, sir! You feel good, huh?"

"I feel like a kid let out of school. Let go the jib halliards, let go the jib halliards, my finger is caught in the block," Mac sang. They rounded the spit that almost landlocked the harbor, and hit the long, smooth swells of the Pacific.

The ocean fought to drag them back to shore, and then, as they hit what the surf-riders call *zeor* in Hawaii, fought to take them out again, away from land. A seagull flew cawing over Mac's head, fluttered down near Tom, and then settled in the rigging. The Filipino took over the bow watch, and Mac went to sit on the grating near Tom.

He was silent for a while. "Tom," he said, finally, "I've got the feeling this is going to be the first unsuccessful McNally trip. I'm having too much fun to make money."

"If they pay money for swimming, diving, you'll show a profit on those girls, sir."

"Still got your mind on them, eh?" McNally looked upon the snub-nosed profile of his boy, standing against the wheel. "You make it sound like white-slavery, Tom."

"Oh, no, sir. Those are good girls, Mr. McNally. They never even see a man till they go home."

Mac whistled. "Tom, sometimes I wonder about what goes on in your mind," he said, "and sometimes I don't wonder, because I'm afraid I'm right…. According to our maps, we put in at a trading port in a couple of days."

"Morning after tomorrow, sir. A French port. Then we skip back to touch at the Moro country. That's pretty wild, sir. We'd better keep the rifles under the hatch."

"I was there ten years ago, when your brother sailed with me. I had quite a crew in those days; I was new to the business, thought I ought to ship a schooner crew. This way, Tom, if we don't get anything, we won't be out much. I would have had to take a vacation anyway, after landing in Frisco from that Aleutian joint…" Mac rolled over on his elbow, and watched the profile of his mate. "Think I'll skip the pearl islands. That business sounds a little more like work than I care for."

The profile jerked. "You would make a grave mistake, Mr. McNally."

"Yeah, I guess so. Well, let it go. There won't be anything at that French port, but we might pick up a few animals at the Moro joint. Say, Tommy, who's going to do the cooking, you or Cecil?"

"I will, sir. I'm a very good cook; our father, you know, has a restaurant."

"God's gift to the homeless wanderer, that's what you are, Tom. I'll take the wheel, go below and dish me up some spaghetti, kid. I've got a little bet with myself."

HE STOOD UP at the binnacle, feeling good, liking the roll of the ketch under his feet, the sight of the stars over his head, the feel of the wheel in his hands. Tom came back in twenty minutes with a bowl of something that made the gray-haired Filipino in the bow jump. "Here it is, sir."

His nostrils twitching, Mac accepted the bowl and a fork and spoon from Tom, and sat crosslegged on the grating, eating. He had been right; this was even better spaghetti than the older brother had cooked. "Tom, remember to tell me to put you in my will.... You leave some for Cecil?"

"Yes, sir."

"Well, I'll relieve him before he jumps out of his skin from the smell."

That night he slept as he hadn't in years; everything was so smooth, so nice. He knew he was riding for a fall, but it didn't matter. In the amusement-procuring trade, you took them as they came. He awoke and ate canned herring-roe and scrambled eggs and golden toast and coffee for breakfast.

"In a family like yours, Tom, I don't see why you aren't all millionaires."

"My father is, sir. Frank and Larry are still young."

"Ugh! My mistake." He moved up on the bench and went to sleep; awoke to take a short watch while each of his men ate, then went back to sleep again; ate a marvelous dinner that started off with tinned turtle soup, and turned in early. Now that they were well out from shore, they didn't bother with a new watch.

Tom woke him in the morning. "We are lying outside the harbor, Mr. McNally, waiting for the tide."

Mac rolled out, shaved, ate, and went up to take charge. But it wasn't necessary; when the tide rose, Tom took her through the opening in the coral reef, and old Cecil tied up neatly enough to a buoy.

A motor launch had already put out from shore. Mac tried to remember the name of the French administrator in this port from ten years ago; but when the launch came near, its tricolor flapping in the breeze, he saw this Frenchman was too young to have been here so long.

The administrator swung aboard, said: "American? I am Monsieur Daugnard, *adminstrateur,* this is Dr. Noyes, our medical officer." Noyes was a halfbreed.

"Gentlemen!" Mac shook hands, introduced himself. "I'm chartering this ship, the crew there—Cecil—owns it."

"The Filipino?"

Mac nodded. "The other boy is working directly for me. He's down on the papers as mate."

"No disease?" Noyes asked.

Mac shook his head. "No, but we'd better prevent any. You gentlemen care for a spot of whisky?"

"But of course," the administrator said. "Why else would he come out?"

Laughing they went below. Tom was ahead of them,

with the siphon and the bottle and three shining glasses set out on the table. Mac poured, and then, for some reason or other, said: "Get yourself a glass, Tom, and have one with us."

"Yes, sir." The boy reached behind the cupboard door.

Mac caught a look at Noyes' face, and cursed himself for a fool. No halfbreed likes to be invited to drink with a native. Tom had already poured himself a small drink; he lifted it, saying: "Your health, gentlemen," and went on deck.

IN THE SILENCE that followed, Daugnard sipped, the other two men avoided each other's eyes. Finally, Daugnard said: "We had a favor to ask you, Mr. McNally."

"Anything," Mac said.

"Two of your compatriots are stranded on an island about forty miles from here. We don't happen to have a boat and a crew able to make the voyage just now. I wonder—you have an extra cabin, haven't you?"

"Yes, but I'm on a long voyage. Two or three weeks. These people may not care for that sort of thing."

"Well," Noyes cut in, "it isn't an emergency. The trading schooner'll get 'em next month."

"Not an emergency of the body, but of the nerves," Daugnard said. "These Americans were making a pleasure trip through the islands. Their boat hit a reef, sank. They sent us a message by a native canoe, but I do not blame them for not wishing to put to sea in one; anyway, they probably couldn't handle it. And I think you would find them amusing, Mr. McNally."

Mac was in a good-natured mood. "All right. There's

plenty of room on the ketch. I'll get the chart, and you can show me where they are."

"I'll come with you," Daugnard said. Together they walked up to the tiny chart house behind the wheel. Tom and Cecil were busy furling the sails.

Daugnard and Mac bent their heads over the map; it took the Frenchman about five minutes to find the position. He marked it on the map, finally, and then straightened up. "You have been in America lately?"

McNally nodded. "About two weeks ago. Why?"

"You are lucky. To see the land of your birth, that is happiness. Me, I have not been home in three years; I must serve two more here. And with no company but that Noyes."

McNally kept a noncommittal silence.

"To me," Daugnard said, "a little dark blood—it is nothing. Do I worry about that? No. But Noyes thinks I do. He thinks all the time that I consider myself better than he because he is a halfbreed. That is not the reason I do not like him. And—"

There was a yell on deck, running feet. They turned, went forward to where Noyes, wavering a little on his feet, was facing Tom Panaki. The doctor's hand was a flail, slashing at Tom's face.

The Kanaka boy was standing perfectly still, a polishing rag in one hand. His skin was so dark that no flush or paleness showed and McNally couldn't tell whether the boy was coldly angry or hotly resentful. He would have preferred the latter.

Mac ran forward, caught the doctor's arm, swung him around. "What the hell do you think you're doing?"

"This fellow didn't move aside when I came along. Teach him a lesson," Noyes said. "He's not in Hawaii now; out here, natives jump when a white man goes by."

Tom said to McNally: "Sir, I—"

"I know, Tom. Go aft, boy."

Daugnard went below, came up with the whisky bottle; it was empty. The administrator held it aloft a moment, then tossed it overboard. "I am sorry, Mr. McNally."

"Okay," Mac said. "Just get him off my boat."

Daugnard bowed. "You'll need to replenish your water. If you will tie up at the pier, I will send a tank down. And I would be honored if you would dine with me."

"So you're not going to punish that boy, eh?" Noyes asked, thickly. "Don't think I'm good—"

"Come along, Noyes," Daugnard said, wearily. "We must go ashore."

He half pulled, half dragged the doctor overside into the launch.

McNally watched them beating back to shore. Then he called: "Tom?"

THE BOY WAS at his shoulder instantly. "Start up the auxiliary, and run into the pier. We might as well get some water. High tide's tonight at ten—so the administrator tells me. We'll have to lay over till then. I don't want you going ashore. Understand?"

Something was choking the Kanaka's throat. "Yes—sir."

Suddenly McNally swore, swore long and hard, with long involved expressions that he hardly believed he knew. He caught himself, stopped, put his hand on Tom's shoulder. "Boy, I wouldn't have had this happen for the world.

But it has happened, and that half breed medico can make trouble for us. So let it go, boy."

Tom's face was smooth. "Yes, Mr. McNally. You can trust me. It is nothing."

"Okay, boy." Mac guided the boat to the wharf while Tom ran the auxiliary. Then he tried to rest on the deck, but it was too hot in the harbor. Palms on the atoll nearly cut all breeze off from the sea. McNally pulled on a fresh white coat over his bare chest and dirty ducks, and went ashore.

The street rose in a hill from the wharf and he paused at the top to look back. Tom Panaki was working around the deck, opening the water tanks. The casks of fresh water came up the other side of the hill to McNally, pulled by a crew of French-chattering natives. Dave went on. He had a vermouth cassis—warm—in a bar, and turned over some stale French and American magazines, and talked awhile to a gendarme who had once served in Africa—he was an Indo-Chinese—then turned back to the waterfront as night began to fall. The street was quiet.

Tom Panaki was sitting on the forecastle hatch, chatting to two native girls who lounged against the bulkhead of the pier. He jumped up as McNally appeared.

"As you were," Mac called, chuckling. "You're seeing the world, Tommy."

Tom Panaki smiled, his white teeth flashing through the gloom, and then went on chatting to the girls in high-school French.

In his cabin, Mac found fresh whites and clean shoes and linen laid out for him. Tom must have overheard the administrator's invitation to dinner. He started to dress, then stopped, staring in the mirror.... Tom had been polishing brass when he and the Frenchman had talked in the chart house.

McNally was still frowning as he went above again. "Ask your friends aboard for dinner, Tom," he called. "You can break out a bottle of wine if you want to, but don't give them any hard liquor." He wanted the boy to forget the insult of the afternoon, wanted to show him that he, McNally, appreciated Tom's education and worth. Then he forgot all about the incident as he went up the hill, through a street become glamorous with lamplight and humming voices from the native huts, passed the same bar he had been in that afternoon, and almost turned in, because it looked so inviting by palm-oil light.

But Noyes was sitting in the bar drinking, and McNally didn't want to see Noyes. He walked on, to the administration building, where the tricolor of France had just been lowered for nightfall. The Frenchman gave him a very poor Martini, and they began dinner.

They were up to the fish of a formal French meal when one of Daugnard's servants clattered outside. Voices were raised, and then Noyes appeared in the doorway that led out to the court. "Sneaking off to have dinner by yourselves?" he asked unpleasantly. "Isn't the medical officer of this—"

He never got to finish his title. His knees folded under him, and his hand let go of the door frame, and he started to fall. McNally had a queer thought—he remembered a drunk like that falling in Australia once, in a dance hall, and a woman had come and picked his pockets while sheepmen and bushrats stepped over the body without looking. Must remember to tell that to—

His train of thought stopped abruptly and he stared. Drinking does not put a knife between a man's shoulder blades. Drinking does not cause red blood to trickle down a white-coated spine, hiding the spots on a linen coat.

MCNALLY SPRANG OVER the body and into the court. Coming out of the light, he couldn't see very much; all he saw was a native figure—that is, a dark figure, naked to the waist—darting into the street. He shouted, "Hey, police," and ran after it.

In the archway, he got another glimpse; the native had a red hibiscus in his hair. Then the man disappeared between two buildings, and McNally, running in pursuit, collided with his friend, the Indo-Chinese cop, and they both fell down, and after that there was not much use chasing the man.

McNally went back into the courtyard, back to the door to the dining room. Daugnard had straightened up. "Dead," he said, without expression. "Let us go down to your boat, McNally."

Dave McNally said: "I know what you're thinking, but it isn't so. Tom isn't a killer."

"Of course. We shall not ask you to take any part in prosecuting him. He is your employee, your friend."

"Let's go," Mac said, between his teeth.

They marched down to the boat, still tied up at the wharf. Music drifted from it as they came up; a girl was singing. "I told Tom he could entertain at a little dinner party," McNally said, without smiling. "It's still going on, I guess."

Their feet clattered on the deck, and when they went into the forecastle, the natives were still. Cecil still held a stringed instrument in his hand; one of the girls had her lips parted, as though she had stopped in the middle of a song. Tom and the other girl were lounging on a locker, their shoulders touching. Tom stood up when they came in.

He was, perhaps, breathing a little hard, but then he had been singing. He said: "Sir?"

"Noyes has been killed," McNally said quickly.

Daugnard cut him short with a movement of his right hand. "You have been on this boat all evening?"

"Yes, sir. Mr. McNally ordered me to stay aboard."

The two girls chattered corroboration in their battered French. Cecil said: "Yes, sar. Tom, he never stir foot all night."

"These damn' natives always stick together," Daugnard said, peevishly. "Where's your knife, boy?"

"I don't own one, *m'sieu*," Tom said. "There's knives on the boat. You want me to fetch—"

"Peculiar that a sailor would not carry a knife," Daugnard said.

"He's not a sailor, he's just out of high school," McNally said, irritably.

Daugnard said: "There is not a choice. I did not like Noyes, but I am administrator. Arrest him."

The Indo-Chinese moved forward, grabbed Tom's wrist. One of the girls began to cry.

The gendarme tugged, and Tom was taken ashore. Daugnard followed without saying goodbye to McNally. The American lit a cigarette, frowned at it without knowing he did, and then said, abruptly, "Stop crying, girl. Do you know where the jail is?"

She stopped, her eyes bright with unshed tears. She nodded.

"It'll be bamboo and mud," McNally said. "All right. Wait a half an hour, and take me there. The boy's a friend of mine." He had, in his life, done worse things, more foolish ones, but never with so little reason.

3

THE TOWN HAD very few alleys; it was so small that all
the houses were on one street. But behind the east row
of houses there was a stream, and behind the west row
there was a desolate waste of refuse dumps. Mac chose the
garbage dumps first, and he and the girl went prowling up
them, bent double to escape the bright moonlight.

But dogs came and whined and snapped at their heels,
and finally, when one of them pursued them persistently,
baying and howling, McNally whispered: "We better cross
over."

"*Tant mieux,*" the girl whispered back, nodding. They
went between two palm-and-mud huts, put so close
together that they could, at one time, hear a man snoring
in one hut and a woman softly humming to a fretful baby
in the other.

The street was deserted. As they hurried across it, Mac
stole a glance up the hill at the town's one light; there was
a policeman there, his white shorts and khaki shirt and
solar topee plainly outlined. It was not the Indo-Chinese
he had talked to that day; and Mac began to fidget a little.
If the colonial was guarding the jail, this business would
run into trouble—serious trouble.

Sneaking for the stream, he looked at his wrist watch. It
was twenty minutes of ten; just right, exactly right to make

high tide and get away. There was no boat to pursue them; the administrator had said as much when he asked them to make the rescue trip.

The girl slid her little hand into Mac's and squeezed. He stopped, put his ear close to her lips.

"*C'est voila,*" she whispered. Her free hand pointed at a house set off on a curve, ahead of them. It was little more than a closet, placed behind another boxlike building; probably the police station.

He marshaled his French, asked the girl whether there would be a guard. She said she didn't know; the gendarmes slept in the front building.

Mac groaned, but he had come this far; he might as well go ahead with it. He had brought a marlin-spike and a heavy knife from the ship.

He had to splash uphill through the stream. As much as possible, he avoided lifting his feet; this was old stuff, he had tracked enough wild animals in his time.

Then, dragging himself out of the stream, flat on his belly so the water from his clothes would not splash on the ground, he made it to the jail wall.

The girl was unconcernedly wringing out her skirt.

As soon as he touched the wall, he knew he could get through. He attacked with the marlin-spike, digging hard, throwing his shoulders into it; he wasn't making much more noise than a rat.

From a barred window, Tom said: "Sir, pass me the knife, I shall dig from inside."

Mac grunted. There was no excitement in Tom's voice, none in the girl's bearing. It seemed as though he, McNally, was the only one who felt fear; and he was supposed to be the leader.

The marlin-spike bit into the wall. Once McNally stopped, his heart rising, cold, into his throat; the off-duty cop had turned over on his cot in the station, was muttering something in his sleep. But the knife inside the jail did not stop grinding.

How did Tom know that McNally would bring an extra knife? How did Tom know a lot of the things he seemed to know? There was something damned odd about Tom. McNally, his wrist and forearm aching from effort, sank back on his haunches. It occurred to him that it might be a good idea to sneak away the way he had come, and leave the Kanaka in there.

"Sir, hurry," Tom said. "The tide will be best in ten minutes."

MCNALLY GRUNTED AND dug away again at the mud mortar. Three minutes later Tom said: "All right, sir. The block that has the bars imbedded in it is loose; I can push it out. Sir, you had better start for the boat."

"Okay, Tommy." McNally shoved the marlin-spike in his belt, made tracks for the stream. He had slid into it, was started down hill when there was a crash behind him; a soft crash.

He didn't stop. He had given Tom the break; let him do the rest. But no rifle fire split the night; the Indo-Chinese must be a heavy sleeper.

A figure caught up to him in the stream, wading along with ease. Tom reached over and took the marlin-spike from McNally and, without the weight, the American went faster.

Where the stream fanned out into the harbor they waded ashore, hurried down the sand to the pier. Cecil was waiting for them. McNally hurried aboard, feeling tired, a little frightened, now that it was all over.

Tom was saying goodbye to the girl who had helped them make the jail break. Then the Kanaka stepped aboard, throwing the hawser off the bitts as he came. "Sir, I can take her out without the auxiliary," he said, and threw some Spanish words at Cecil.

The ketch slid out into the harbor on the power of her foremast. The tide had reached its peak, was going out again, and that helped them. They floated over the reef without trouble, and Tom handed the wheel to McNally while he went to run up the mains'l.

Looking back, McNally could see the small figure of the girl—on the pier. She was waving.

Tom secured the mainsail, came back to the wheel. "Sir, we are free. I thank you." Then he said, "Sir, that girl wanted to sail with us. I had a little trouble with her."

"Tom," McNally said, "You're a cold bird. But don't get too big for your wing spread.... Tom, I suppose an Eagle Scout like you knows all about radio code. Run that receiving set off the batteries, and stand by to get any messages about chasing us. I don't want any French destroyers putting wheels over our bows."

"Sir, very good. But, sir, I do not think there will be pursuit. Monsieur Daugnard wanted me to get away."

"How do you know, Tom?"

"Sir, I just know."

"You just know too much," McNally grunted, and went below to get out of his wet clothes and into his bunk.

He slept, though he hadn't thought he would. He slept till the smell of breakfast woke him up. He went up on deck in his pajamas. It was a fine clear day, but aft there was a smudge on the horizon that diminished while he watched.

Tom brought him breakfast, followed his eyes. "Sir, that was lucky for us, that was a hurricane. But it missed us, sir. However, I am afraid it has already grounded the trading schooner."

"Eh?"

"The radio, sir. Also, there will be no pursuit. Daugnard sent a message to Tahiti concerning the incident, and said that he could not identify the boat, as Noyes was port officer, and had kept no record of the ketch. So you see, sir, we are all right. Daugnard wanted us to escape. I think, too, sir, we shall have to take the American ladies with us to the pearl islands; they had better not return to French territory."

Dave said: "What? American ladies?"

"Yes, sir, the ones that you promised Monsieur Daugnard to rescue. With the trading schooner laid up, they would be there for months. It's no place for women."

"Oh, yeah…. But, Tommy, Daugnard didn't say they were *women.*"

"I heard it back there in—" Tom broke off.

"So you were ashore. You killed Noyes, didn't you, Tom?"

"Sir, those girls were very talkative." Tom was trying to get the subject changed. "The younger American lady—she was engaged to Noyes. Met him in San Francisco, sir, when he was on his vacation, thought he was just sunburned, I guess, sir. Then when she got out, she found out the difference, and—"

"The inquiring reporter, eh, Tom?" McNally looked up at his mate. "Kid, I am captain on this boat. And I am a long-suffering man, but— Watch it, Tom. I'm tough when I'm mad. All right, what time do we pick up these women?"

"About eight bells, sir. I shall attend to everything."

"No," McNally decided. "No, Tom. I've gotten you out of one jail. From now on, my friend, you stand by, and take orders. I shall attend to everything."

"Sir, yes."

4

THERE HAD NEVER been an expedition quite like this before, McNally told himself. This rambling around, getting Kanaka mates out of jail, picking up stranded women, tacking back and forth—he was McNally. And McNally usually went in and drove hard for his destination, his objective, got his prize and went home. Well, sometimes he had to take second prize but this—this conducting a tour of the South Seas for an employee's benefit was childish.

His object was to go take a look at his problematical island, and then either load up the ketch with an exhibit or make the easy leg to the Japanese culture pearl beds and take up six Jap girls for a swimming team.

But all these other things seemed to be proper at the time. Maybe they would all come out in a plan, maybe there was some rhyme or reason to them. Yeah, maybe.

But at a little before eight bells, when they made their landfall, he went below and changed into clean ducks.

And he took up the master's position beside the wheel because, in his heart, he knew a man looked impressive there. Cecil handled the wheel and Tom reefed sails. They switched on the auxiliary and went into the harbor smartly.

There was no administration here; no port authority to keep them from tying up to the dock. And there was no dock. So they dropped anchor well out, and Cecil let over the dinghy under Tom's directions. Then Tom rowed McNally to shore.

There was nothing but natives in sight.

McNally caught one of them up, asked him in Lingua Franca about white women. The man grinned, said: "I take. You givem cigarette?"

McNally handed him a cigarette, called to Tom: "I'm going inland, Mr. Panaki. Watch the landing."

Tom saluted from among a knot of admiring native girls. The boy had a way with women.

McNally strolled up the coral shore, towards a group of huts. He was about ten feet from the one his guide indicated when a female voice called: "If you come any farther, I'll shoot."

McNally said: "Hey. This is a friend, come to rescue you, sister." He did not feel as jaunty as he looked.

A brown-haired head stuck out of the door of the hut, and the girl said: "Are you—are you an American?"

"Yeah. Mind if I come in? Emily Post says—"

The girl came out. "What are you doing here? I didn't know any steamers ever—"

"I've got a ketch in the harbor. Daugnard sent me to rescue you." McNally coughed. "He said there were two—"

"My aunt left. She hired a war-canoe to take her to—"

Something crawled up McNally's spine. "There's an old nautical saying," he grunted. "One woman on a ship, or one priest. You haven't got a priest?"

"What?" This was a pretty girl, all right. It would be. But there was a small, tight look around her eyes that he didn't like.

"Let it go. If you'll pack your pretties, I'll send my mate up to get them."

"How do you know I'm going with you?"

"Sister, it is nothing to me. But—as the French say— nothing. Only—if you just want the luxury of debating awhile, you're going to be out of luck. We came in just below high tide, according to my books, and we go out just after it. If we stay any longer, my first mate kills people. He calls it landsickness."

"Are you making any sense at all, Mr.—"

"McNally's the name. And I don't know if—"

Dave McNally reeled over, went down. As some nice, tropical blackness cut off his sight, it occurred to him that white men don't go wading in tropical streams after dark without chewing hopefully on a lot of quinine.

"There's no dusk in the tropics," he said, from the ground.

WHEN HE CAME to, he was on the ketch, and they were out to sea. His ears rang like a carrillon; he turned over in his bunk, groaning. A hand put a cold towel on his forehead, said: "Drink this."

The stuff was cold beef bouillon, mixed with evaporated milk. He drank it, felt strong enough to sit up. The girl shoved a pillow under his shoulders.

"Boy," McNally said. "That was a bad one. Fever."

"Yes, I know. Mr. Panaki tells me you are just down from the Arctic, too."

"Yeah. I've had fever before, and it backs up on you. Hey, thanks for taking care of me. I'd better get on deck and set a course."

He tried to sit up.

"Mr. Panaki said to make you rest if I had to—had to

sit on you. He's very devoted to you…. By the way, thank you for rescuing me. I was getting very sick of that island. Mr. Pa—"

McNally said: "Call him Tom. My name is Dave McNally. We're informal on this ketch."

"Oh. My name's Lucia. Lucia Bradford."

"Nice name," McNally said. "All right, Lucia. Come on and sit on me. I'm going up on deck and find out where we're going. Tom Panaki has ideas occasionally."

"He's very well educated," Lucia said, putting a hand on Mac's head and pushing him down. "I shall write an article about him for the Normal School Review. My aunt and I were making a tour of the South Seas to study educational conditions here. We ran into—"

Mac whistled. "All right, girl," he said, "anything you say." He took her hand from his forehead, and swung out of the berth.

She grabbed his arm, pulled herself close to him in the cabin. "Don't you believe me?"

"What difference does it make?" he asked. "I'll drop you off within a couple of days and—"

She said: "All right. You met Dr. Noyes back at—"

He said, heavily: "I know the story. You were engaged to him, and didn't know he was a—"

She said: "Yes."

He did not look at her.

"You know Noyes is dead?"

"Mr. Panaki told me. He was killed in a drunken fight, he said. Mr. Panaki said—"

"Mr. Panaki is too damned smart," Dave McNally

growled, and swung away from the girl. He slammed the cabin door behind him, tore up on deck.

Cecil was at the wheel, his wizened little face intent on the compass. Tom Panaki was working around, whistling. He saw Mac, and carefully lashed the rope he had been trimming before hurrying over.

"Sir, you should be below. Fever, sir, is—"

"Is over," Mac said. He did feel rocky, but he made it to the wheel. He leaned over the chart table. He swore.

"Hey, Tom! Who laid this course, you? You've passed up my island altogether. How long was I out of my head?"

"Two days, sir. Miss Lucia has been devoted, she has nursed you every moment."

"Nuts with Miss Lucia," McNally snapped. "We're nearly onto the pearl bed islands. Whose idea was that, yours?"

"Sir, yes. With you incapacitated, I deemed it best to beat for the port where your trip was sure to become a financial success, instead of loitering in the roadway off a problematical island which might net you nothing of a commercial nature."

"You're taking too much on yourself," McNally said. He braced himself against the charthouse wall, digging his bare heels into the holes in the grating to keep himself upright. "I'm in command here, I am the charterer of this ship, and I am your boss."

He wondered whether he had strength enough to take the Kanaka if it came to a fight, and rather doubted it. Tom's smooth skin covered an awful lot of muscle, and anyway, the boy had probably taken a Merit Badge in jiu-jitsu.

BUT MCNALLY REACHED behind him and got hold of the heavy metal ruler they used to chart the courses. He'd get in a couple of whacks, anyway. His speculative eye took in the wiry little Filipino's back. Cecil might jump either way, but probably he would jump for McNally's throat.

But it didn't come to a fight. Tears welled into Tom Panaki's velvet eyes. "Sir, if you do not trust me, make Cecil mate and I shall serve as deckhand. Mr. McNally, I am heartbroken."

"All right, all right. But I want to make it to that island. We'll change the course and—"

"Sir," Tom Panaki said, "that would be a grievous waste of time. Look, sir—if I may be permitted—let me show you on the chart. I do not intend to presume but—"

"Out with it, man, out with it." But McNally knew he was licked. He turned, rolling his shoulders along the charthouse wall to keep himself standing upright.

Tom Panaki eagerly brought the chart over for McNally to see. "Sir, our course homeward could cut right past the island without a moment's waste of time. You see—"

"Yeah," McNally said bitterly. "But if I've got a shipload of Japanese swimming girls on board, where am I going to carry any exhibits I get on the island? That's why I wanted to play for the big show first."

"Oh, sir, I am sorry, but I feared that you would wish to shorten the trip because of your illness, and I wished to insure you against loss. Oh, I have been presumptuous; my father and my brother Larry frequently have chided me for it."

"Ah, nuts," McNally said. His head was still ringing, and the motion of the boat made him sick. "From now on, boy, if there are any decisions to make, I make them, if you have to douse me over the side to bring me to. I've fought," McNally said, "in every latitude and longitude on this earth. From Hey Rubes in Iowa to bandits in the Caucasus, from cannibals in Borneo to headhunters in Africa. I've been in eight revolutions," Dave McNally shouted, and his head went around and his knees buckled, "three wars, five race riots, and so many fights that I'm scar tissue from the Achilles tendon on my right heel to the mastoid bone on my left ear. I—"

The girl's head appeared from below, and she got one arm while Tom got the other, and he could feel the soles of his feet bumping against the treads as they took him below. His bed was very soft, for a moment, and then the chill that followed the fever caught him in its grip, and ice made his eyes ache and his belly collapse, and he was dimly conscious of blankets and more blankets, and Lucia and Tom bending over him with hot tea and strong bouillon.

5

THIS WAS A polite voice, but it hissed. So it was not Tom, nor was it Lucia. The voice said: "This will make you better in a half an hour, sir," and then hissed some more.

A needle pricked his arm. He said: "Thanks, Doctor," and lay very still, and gradually the ringing went away, and he could sit up and be surprised that the doctor was a woman: a muscular little Japanese woman of about fifty years.

"That has been one of the worst bouts of fever I have ever seen, Captain McNally," the doctor said. "Your mate informs me that you have been in the Arctic, following fever in Asia?"

"Yes, Doctor."

"Well, it will be safe for you to land. I should take it easy a few days."

"You speak very good English, Doctor."

"I was educated at Vassar and the College of Physicians and Surgeons at Columbia University," the doctor said.

"Congratulations." Mac started to get out of the bunk, and then realized that he was not dressed. "I should like to dress," he said. "And you're sure it's all right for me to land? I don't want to start an epidemic on your island."

"Oh, thank you very much, Captain, but this disease is

spread only by mosquitoes, of which we have none. You, sir, were bitten years ago, and the virus remains in your blood."

"It seems to be getting worse, though," Mac said. "I can't remember a bout like this before."

"You must take better care of yourself. I shall see you ashore, then." The doctor paused in the doorway. "You are not, by any chance, a Columbia man, Captain?"

"Sorry, I never went to college."

"So sorry," the Japanese woman said, and went above.

When McNally came on deck, Lucia, dressed in faded blue shorts and a faded blue denim sailor blouse, was perched on the edge of the dock. Cecil was standing anchor guard. "How do you feel, sailor?" the girl asked.

"Okay. Thanks for all the care I got."

She walked over, took his arm. "You made wild and passionate love to me during one phase of it," she said, smiling. "Tom was quite embarrassed. Unfortunately, you didn't use my right name, even once. I'm afraid you've got a past, Dave."

"Yeah, probably." He jumped ashore. "I've got a vague idea that I've been pushed around a good deal," he said. "Whatever it was that doctor gave me has fixed me up again, and I've a couple of accounts to settle with Mr. Thomas Panaki. From being a vague notion of how to insure my trip, this pearl culture business has become the main objective. I gather that's where we are."

She nodded. "That's right. Dr. Tangi said to bring you to her house for cocktails. Afterwards, we're going to see the girls dive, and then you can talk business with the manager tonight."

"That's as good a reason as any for not doing any of those

things," McNally said. "I've done too many things in the last few days that I didn't intend to. It's about time I got the reins back in my own hands. Where's Tom?"

"The manager loaned him a handcart and a tank to get water for the ketch. There isn't a hose line down to the dock."

McNally grunted. He couldn't complain about that. The mate's duty was to get water as soon as they landed, in case the captain wanted to sail immediately. But he was going to have a showdown with Mr. Panaki, and that soon. He and the girl strolled inland.

LUCIA SAID: "YOU must think I'm an awful fool. Falling for Dr. Noyes. But he had glamour and a sort of charm, and I was a school teacher, with nothing to look forward to but more school teaching, and I didn't know he was a—" She paused, blushed.

"Look," Mac said, "don't get British, just because you've been living where they wear sun helmets. I've got nothing against Noyes for being half-Polynesian, and there's nothing wrong with him. No, it wasn't that, it was that he was such a drunken, dull sort of—"

"But he behaved in San Francisco."

"Yeah, I suppose so. Say, this is quite a place."

It was. Superimposed on the South Seas luxury of plants and trees, coconuts and flowers was a Japanese neatness, a care that emphasized the lushness of the place. Each path was carefully marked, weedless and spotless, each flower had a cup cut in the earth around it—but the flowers were ten times the size of any Japanese bloom. Ahead of them, two girls in middy-blouses and voluminous bloomers were sweeping a path, three others were building a rock-and-cement bridge across a little stream.

"Lovely," Lucia said.

There was a rumbling noise, and Tom came around the bend in the path, preceding a water cart drawn by a half dozen giggling girls in the same strangely American costume. Tom himself was not lending a hand; this was the island where women did the work.

Tom saluted McNally. "Sir, I am a great success here."

"You always will be," McNally said, sourly. "Get that water aboard, and stand by the boat."

The boy did not look crestfallen. "Sir, as you say. But, I have been invited to cocktails at Madame, the Doctor's."

"You're coming up in the social scale, Tom. But I'll make your apologies for you."

"Sir, if I may presume, it would not be wise. The Japanese are very touchy as to color prejudice in the East; Madame might misconstrue your motives in not having me attend—"

McNally barked: "You work for me. Do as I say!"

Tom saluted. "Aye, aye, sir." He went down the path with his girls.

"But he was right," Lucia said. "If you hurt the Japanese's feelings—"

"They might take Manchuria away from me," Mac snapped. "Yeah, I know." He felt silly, as though he had been guilty of schoolboy temper, of childish petulance. "Come on, let's get along to this party."

They went and the party was dull. The doctor and Lucia discussed educational affairs in the United States; once Mac cut in: "Talking about Columbia, do you remember when the Columbia was the big spot of the burlesque circuit?" but they stared at him as though he were a noisy boy.

He strolled to the window of the doctor's little paper-and-glass house, and whistled. Eight girls had lined up outside; which was not strange, in an island populated only by women. Only—the eight girls were wearing web cartridge belts around the tops of their bloomers, and there were nasty looking .45s in the belts.

The little doctor came over to him. "Yes, Mr. McNally," she said, looking out the window. "Our island police. Won't you come have another drink? I'm sure it will do you no harm."

"You're the doctor," he said unhappily. They went back to the cocktail table, and once again he kneeled on the floor. **THE DOCTOR SAID:** "Miss Lucia, you would not mind? Will you step in the next room, through that door there, and get me my Columbia yearbook? I want to see if you recognize anyone I know—"

The girl smiled, and got up to go get the book. Dave McNally said sharply: "But there's no room there, that goes—"

"Our Japanese architecture is so confusing," the doctor said. "It appears to be simpler than it is." She positively simpered as Lucia stepped through the door, which slid shut behind her.

"Well," the doctor said, "if you won't have a drink, Captain, let us go watch the girls dive. It is a sight that is very, very interesting."

Mac got up, reluctantly, suspiciously. "Hey," he said, "what's going on? Where's the girl?"

"Oh, on this island, we have very many girls," the doctor said, taking Mac's arm. "Come."

He backed away from her. "Those lady cops out there have pinched Lucia," he accused her.

"Oh, yes." The doctor smiled. "But then, what is Miss Lucia to you? You never met her—"

"She's an American," Mac said. He brushed the doctor aside, and rushed for the door.

A girl in a middy blouse that bore three chevrons stepped through it before he got there, and pointed a gun at him. If the girl was small, the gun was not.

Mac stopped, dead. "Okay," he said. His eyes were hard. "You've got me. What's the game? My papers are in order—" he began. Then he stopped. "Your man in Manila was awfully anxious to have me visit here. So what do you get out of it?"

"Oh," the doctor said, "please come and see the diving girls. I am only the doctor; the manager handles all that sort of thing. Please, do not make any trouble."

Mac said, pleasantly: "All right, I won't," and made a dive for the girl with the gun.

It was the first time this trip that he felt at home, and that was funny, because he had seldom, if ever, wrestled with a girl before, and certainly never with one so small. As his big fingers closed on the sergeant's wrist, she fired; but the bullet went high, broke tile in the doctor's roof.

The little doctor was hammering on his skull with a cloisonne vase.

The sergeant was strong for a girl. But a shove on her biceps, and her fingers opened, and McNally had the gun. He backed off, breathing hard, not from exertion. "Take me to somebody who can explain this hunk of piracy to me," he ordered the little doctor.

"Oh, please, Mr. McNally," she said. "You shouldn't have done that. That poor girl may kill herself with disgrace now."

"Cut it out," he said. "Cut it out, and now. I'm tired of this tea-party nonsense; I want to know what is going on."

"Sir!" Tom Panaki wailed behind him. "You have spoiled everything."

McNally turned, saw the gun in Tom's hand, brought his own gun around to bear on his mate. The sergeant girl hit him full in the face with a tea table; she was fast as light.

He staggered, and they had the gun. Tom's gun covered one side, the sergeant's the other; there was not much use in doing anything but stand still.

"Please, Mr. McNally," the doctor said. "You will come see the diving girls?"

6

THE LITTLE DOCTOR tripped along at McNally's side, holding on to his tensed forearm. Behind, the polite Tom had given his arm to the sergeant; they carried the guns. McNally walked because he had to, and he kept his mouth shut. His thoughts would have passed no censor.

Tommy, my boy—he thought—if I ever get you to sea again, I'm going to take the brown hide off you in strips. You—you Eagle Scout you. I'm going to keelhaul, plank-walk and bilge you, you polite buzzard.

McNally turned his head. "Done your good deed lately, Tom?"

"Sir, every day I do a good deed. Please, sir, do not misunderstand my actions; the girl, Miss Lucia, was not of a high type. She—"

"Was not? Was not? If you and your polite little chums have hurt her, you'll—"

"It is not as you think, sir. There—"

"Please, the manager will discuss business," the doctor said. "If you do not mind, Mr. Panaki."

"Eagle Scout Panaki," McNally said, nastily. "Were you a patrol-leader, too, Tom?"

"I am still Assistant Scout Master of my old troop," Tom said, proudly. "I do not see what my scouting activities have to do, sir, with the present situation."

"Please, gentlemen, do not argue," said the doctor. "Here are the diving girls. This is a sight, please, which you should observe closely; very, very few men ever see it."

"No, but I had to be lucky," McNally said. "Lucky McNally, that's me."

Against his will, the showman had to stop and admire. The girls on the dock, in the boats, were Japanese, to be sure; they had the short figures, the foreshortened legs, of their race. But what builds.

"Now, please," the doctor said. "Observe. The girls on the dock are preparing to dive by doing their breathing exercises. Please, you have a watch, Mr. McNally?"

"Yeah, but I'm not going to loan it for any tricks," McNally grated.

The doctor smiled her polite smile, and called aloud in Japanese. A girl came over, stood at attention in front of them. But her eyes drifted sidewise to rest on Tom. The Kanaka boy colored; scouting had not prepared him for the girl's costume.

"If you will time this girl's breathing, Mr. McNally," the doctor said. "Please, you will observe that our girls can hold their breaths for six minutes and over. Please, you will say ready, Mr. McNally."

The girl was turning her arms out, hands against her sides, slowly expanding her chest. McNally waited till the second hand came around to the top, said: "Ready."

The girl took a deep breath and stood still.

After that, time seemed to catch itself by the forelock and stand still. The second hand went around and around, and the girl just stood there, not moving, not breathing; she seemed to lose the semblance of life and become a statue, and her costume was right, correct.

When the little hand had passed zero four times, McNally cried: "Tell her to breathe!"

The doctor smiled; the girl's face was not red yet. Another minute went by, and a sixth one; Tom Panaki was catching his breath in little gasps, and McNally's heart was pounding; the girl seemed to be smiling a little. At six minutes and twelve seconds she let her wind out, and the world moved again.

The girl regained her breath easily, without panting.
"IT IS EASIER, please," the doctor said, "when one is not working. Now, this girl will get her boat and her partner, and show us the oysters she nurses." She gave the girl—child, really—an order in Japanese.

They all got into the row boat and went out, the girl rowing, her partner watching through a glass-bottomed bucket. The oarsman's muscles rippled smoothly, like a race horse, as she sent the boat forward in long sweeps, McNally said, "Six of them on a stage—"

The watcher called out, and the girl shipped the oars. There were buoys all around; the girls lashed the boat to one of them, and the girl who had been rowing stood up, took her breathing exercises again.

Then she cried something in Japanese, and went over the side. When she hit the water not a teacup full was splashed.

They leaned over the side and watched her go down the buoy anchor rope. Her assistant was laying out tools on the sternboard.

The buoy rope jerked, and the assistant promptly lowered

a net-bag full of tools over. There was a stone attached to take them down.

"We have tried diving helmets," the doctor said, "but they are not so good. The girls cannot be delicate with their fingers, and the oysters die. You see, what we do is this—we bore a hole in a young oyster, and insert a speck of—well, a speck. That is our secret. The oyster immediately begins to make a pearl. But sometimes the hole sickens the oyster; then the girls give it medicine. Sometimes the pearl becomes misshapen; then they do other things. But all this must be done on the floor of the ocean; to move the oyster is to injure it." She took another breath, said: "These oysters are inedible, the edible oyster doesn't grow a commercial pearl. It takes from three to five years to—"

The diving girl broke the surface and climbed easily into the boat, tossing her bobbed hair back out of her eyes.

Her partner stood up, breathed, and went over; the first girl took the glass bucket and went on lookout.

"These girls come to us when they are nine," the doctor said, "and undergo rigorous training. We must weed out those who have any disorder of the heart, lungs or other organs. Those of an unstable disposition are also weeded out, and no men are permitted on the island except the manager. This is because psychological researches have shown us that a girl will steal to give to a man when she will not steal for her own account."

"Did you ever lose any pearls?" McNally asked.

"When we do we spare no trouble to recover them and punish the girl responsible," the doctor said. "As an example; it is easy to identify our pearls, as each bed grows a different type, due to the food we give them, the temperature of the current, and so on.... The girl on the bottom is the junior one of the pair we see working; she does the feeding after this girl here does the doctoring. The oysters are fed with—"

The second girl came up, and McNally said: "I've had enough of this. Let's go see the manager. Every time one of these girls goes under water, I get the jitters."

The doctor said: "Please, it is as you wish." She ordered the girls in Japanese.

They started for shore, each girl now taking an oar.

Halfway in to shore another rowboat came near them, also heading in. The girls in the two boats exchanged laughing words, and then McNally realized that a race had been arranged; the stroke was quickened, the boat went faster than ever.

THE BOAT PULLED neatly alongside the dock, where an instructor in middy blouse and bloomers was giving breathing lessons to little girl apprentices. The senior pearl-nurse leaped out, landing smoothly, put down her hand to help the passengers out. The doctor went first, then McNally.

He tried to avoid the girl's outstretched hand, feeling it humiliating to be hauled up by a woman. But she caught his hand anyway, pulled him up without apparent effort. He stopped next to her, put his hand on her biceps; they were as hard as stone, as sexless as a machine. He understood what the man in Manila had meant by the girls having trouble finding husbands.

He turned. Tom Panaki was communicating with the girl under his breath; the words were in Japanese, McNally couldn't catch them.

He said: "Naughty, naughty, Tom."

The mate blushed again, looked ashamed, "Sir, not as you think, I—"

"The manager will explain to Mr. McNally," the doctor said firmly. "Please, you come, Captain."

"Sure," McNally said. "I guess. It's about time there were some explanations."

They went up a little, neat path; not an ant hole, not a fallen leaf soiled it. Every rock on the island had been brought there from Japan, he knew; every hunk of coral had, apparently, been shaped into something new and moved. The place was like a Japanese garden.

They passed a Shintoist shrine, which some girls were busily redecorating. McNally said: "How many girls on the island?"

"Four hundred on this one. But this is only one plant of our company, and we are not the largest pearl-culture company in Japan. The greatest—"

"Let it go. This Cook's Tour business gets me down. Well, with four hundred, you ought to be able to spare me my six that I want."

"And, sir, here is the manager's house," Tom Panaki said. "Now you will see, I am no villain."

"How did you know this was where the manager lived, then?"

"Sir, the sign over the door says so."

"So you read Japanese, too, Tom? Boy, what an education."

"Sir, thank you for the compliment."

"It wasn't meant as a compliment."

They had to take off their shoes to go into the manager's house; when they put them down, McNally stopped, startled. There were other pairs of shoes there, but one pair in particular interested him—a pair of low heeled slippers, obviously American.

The girl was in here.

The little sergeant had been following discreetly; she took up a position by the shoes. McNally measured the distance to her gun, and let one shoulder down, ready to leap.

Tom Panaki caught him as he took off; the Kanaka's hands grabbed McNally's shoulder. Dave McNally was pulled around, facing his mate; the American's left fist came up, lashed into Tom's face.

The Kanaka took a step backward, and went for his gun. McNally gave up trying to make it for the sergeant; he tackled with Tom Panaki.

Something hit between McNally's shoulder blades, and he thought he was stabbed or shot for a moment. Then the thing moved, and he realized it was the tense, struggling body of the little girl-sergeant.

He twisted his big shoulders, and sent her flying.

TOM PANAKI TOOK advantage of the break to grasp one hand on McNally's throat, the other hand on his own gun. The strong brown fingers cut into his windpipe, and McNally fell.

As he plunged forward he was aware of a lot of things, and not aware of them at the same time. Things like—his ear nearly being torn off—his shirt splitting up the back—a gun roaring. Then a huge shock, and afterwards, somehow, he was up on the porch of the manager's house, staining the oiled paper door with blood from a crushed left arm, and holding Tom Panaki's gun on a crowd of island police-women and on Tom.

"Please," the doctor cried, "you misunderstand, Captain McNally."

He said: "Okay. If anybody comes at me, they'll misunderstand, too."

His stocking foot went through the paper door, ruined it, and he backed up, was in the house. He called: "Lucia! Hey, Lucia!"

She cried: "Yes, yes, this way, McNally."

He plunged through a couple of paper doors and found her.

She had on a Japanese kimono that was too short for her. Her hair was wild. She was standing in a room where sat a man, an aged, almost ageless Japanese man in black silk kimono. He said: "I am the manager, please. You must listen to me, Mr. McNally."

Mac said: "Okay. Stand up, Mr. Manager." He moved behind the man, got him out to the wrecked porch. "Tell that crowd to get a hundred paces from the house and stay there. Quick!"

"With pleasure, Mr. McNally. I am very, very happy to do so." The manager burbled Japanese softly, and the women moved back.

"That," bawled McNally, "means you, too, Tom." He watched the Kanaka walk backwards.

McNally said to the manager: "And to think I cut that guy out of a jail. He was in for murder."

"Which he did not commit," the manager said. "Please, I am very, very sorry we have deceived you, Mr. McNally.

Won't you honor me by coming to my room, and letting me explain."

"And how. Now, Manager, start backing up. My gun's going to be pressing you all the time."

Going that way they crept back to the room where Lucia had been. She was still standing there.

"I don't know why I'm going to all this trouble for you," McNally growled. "Except I figured I was next. What did they do to you?"

"They're crazy women," the girl sobbed. "They took my clothes to search. They—"

"All right," the manager said, "you have said enough, young lady. Mr. McNally, now for the explanations—they would have been forthcoming in any event. You stopped at an island where there was a Dr. Noyes and a Monsieur Daugnard. Right?"

"I like your English," McNally said. "Yeah. Right. Tom killed Noyes."

"But, no," the manager said. "Daugnard killed Noyes. You see, Noyes was a very brave man, and a very bad one. He stole some pearls from us—"

"How? By disguising himself as a diving girl?"

"How cannot be told," the manager said. "That is something we do not want repeated." He looked at the gun in McNally's hand, and said: "Not if you shoot me. One more—mishap of the sort Dr. Noyes committed, and I should be dishonored."

"Hari-kari, eh? Okay, go on. I don't believe a word."

"NOYES WROTE THIS—WROTE Miss Lucia to come visit him," the manager said. "She was to get the pearls back to the States. But the pearls, you see, are partly Monsieur Daugnard's. His share for sheltering Noyes."

"And Daugnard had Noyes killed."

"Yes. Mr. Panaki had persuaded Daugnard that he could keep you in ignorance, make you run the pearls back to Manila for him. Mr. Panaki is a very persuasive young man."

"Yeah. Yeah, I get that. He was working for you, was he?"

"Yes. He has ambitions to be a private detective. You see, everything is neat when you know. By working on you, Mr. Panaki got you to pick up the girl and bring her to us. You are well known, could get the sailing papers and so on."

"Yeah. You got your pearls back?"

"Oh, yes," the manager said. "We have our pearls back. The girl had them."

Dave McNally sat down, the gun dangling between his fingers. He sat on a low tea table, because there were no chairs. Yes, everything had been very neat. Probably—undoubtedly—Tom had given him something to simulate fever. The dirty— He looked at Lucia. "Did you have the pearls?"

"Yes," she said. "But I didn't know they were stolen."

McNally whistled soundlessly between his teeth. "How did you people know I even thought of coming out here? How did you—"

"A bus boy in San Francisco," the manager said. "When you were talking in a restaurant to a friend, Mr. Loeb."

"Yeah, my agent. I suppose you had your men looking all over the Coast for someone who had the idea of coming here. You would." Dave McNally stood up. "Of course, you won't let me sign up the six girls I wanted. That was just a ruse. To get me here."

"Oh, but yes," the manager said. "We are very, very grateful to you. The six girls—they would graduate in a month—are already in the forecastle of your ketch. I have taken the liberty of drawing up contracts, which they signed."

"Well, I'll be a—" McNally stood up. "So long, Manager. Come on, Lucia."

The manager said: "No. The lady stays here."

Mac said: "I knew there was a catch. She goes with me. The good Lord knows I don't want her; when I get her, I'm going to lock her in the spare cabin till we make Manila. But she goes."

The manager said: "No. I am very, very sorry, but—"

Mac caught the old man up, got a half Nelson on him. "I am very, very sorry, too. Let's go. Lucia, get behind me."

MAC FORCED THE old man through the front door. He felt kind of bad about this, but the girl was a fellow countryman, and he couldn't leave her. He made the manager clear a path with his voice; they went through lanes of surly, muttering women.

When they came to the ketch, McNally said: "Lucia, get aboard. Throw off the hawsers."

He knew what this was costing him, knew he was a fool. Tough McNally. But he had to do it. When the girl called: "The hawsers are off, the boat's drifting—" he jumped, kicked the ketch free from the dock, pushed the self starter on the auxiliary, and grabbed the tiller. The manager screamed something, and there were six small splashes as McNally's attraction—his act—swam back to their island. Jake Loeb would think him crazy.

Cecil came pattering aft, said: "Me glad to leave them women. Glad Tom go, too."

"All right, boy, take the wheel." McNally glared at Lucia. "Go below, to the spare cabin, and don't come out till I call." He looked at where Tom Panaki's brown face shone among the yellow ones of the women.

Then he went down to his cabin to get a bandage for his wounded arm. There was a package on the table.

When he opened it, it contained three thousand dollars in American bills—new ones—and a note.

"Sir, I have hated to use you this way. This is your share of my reward for recovering the pearls—it is only fair you do not lose financially on your journey. I trust we shall meet again."

It was, of course, signed with Tom's name.

McNally sighed, went and knocked on Lucia's door. "Come on out," he called. "You're going to have to be cook till we make port."

She appeared, still in the kimono. "Yes, sir." Then she said: "What port are we going to?"

"The way I feel now," McNally said, "any port where I can catch a boat for Alaska."

Then he stared at Lucia for a long moment. "You didn't know those pearls were stolen?"

"No," she said.

THE SINGING CATS OF SIAM

In Siam McNally sought ivory apes and troubadour cats who chanted, "Sing Something Simple." But Siam wasn't simple any more—not since Ling had emigrated from Mott Street

1

THE BOAT PADDLED its way up the river, parting fishing canoes and sailing boats as it went. There were no banks to the river; the water gradually ceased to be water, became swamp, then mud, and then, finally, dirt. On hills above the river were shining temples, and the little people—shiftless as monkeys, and just as gay—waved to the dozen passengers. McNally was telling the girl about the time he had come here after white elephants.

The girl said: "Elephants! White elephants! Now I know you're kidding."

McNally grinned again: "Straight stuff, kid. I'm in show business, collecting acts for sideshows and tours." He rolled a little in the deck chair.

"But they wouldn't sell you a white elephant. The white elephants are sacred."

McNally snorted. "Sure. The history of the Orient, as written by P.T. Barnum. A white elephant is no more sacred to a Siamese than—than a string of pearls like yours to an American."

The girl flushed. Her hand fluttered to her throat, tucked the pearls inside her blouse. "I thought the white elephant were the exclusive property of the royal family."

"Yeah," McNally said. "Of the nobility. Rolls Royces are the exclusive right of millionaires. See?"

"Oh." Without being asked—Dave McNally knew how to mind his own business—she said: "My father's an expeditionary photographer. We travel around and take pictures to sell to magazines."

"Nice for you," McNally said. He cocked a speculative eye at her father, a portly gent in cummerbund and whites, who was having a drink up on the paddle box. "See the world and get paid for it."

"Don't you do that?" she asked.

"Sometimes," McNally said. "Most of the time I'm either in the welldeck of some ship, trying to persuade a sick animal to take castor oil, or I'm in some British official's office, talking him out of having me heaved in the local booby hatch. I don't know," said McNally, "what's so funny about my trade. When vaudeville was going good, there were lots of us scouting around. Not so many, now."

"Well," she said, "there's Frank Buck."

"He's a menagerie man," McNally said. "I'm a showman.

My specialty is getting things that'll perform, do something. Animals or people."

The girl said: "Father, this is Mr. McNally. My father, Mr. Gatrun. Mr. McNally's a showman, daddy, he collects variety acts."

Gatrun's eyes were lean and hungry in his fat face. He studied McNally for a moment, said: "Looking for another pair of Siamese twins, Mr. McNally?"

Dave McNally was still good-natured, though he didn't like Gatrun. Well, the man's daughter was a pretty enough thing to find on a Siamese river boat. "No," he drawled. "One of my scouts told me there were four Siamese cats up the river here that had been trained to sing like a quartet. I'm having a look. If they aren't up to expectations, I can show some profit on a few albino apes."

Gatrun's face tightened, and McNally saw for a moment that the man was not so fat as he looked. He was muscular, beefy, not soft at all. His heavy face slowly flushed, and he said: "Very interesting. Very, very interesting. Albino apes, eh?"

There was trouble here. Well, it was the trouble you ran into that kept the suckers out of this business. Dave McNally said: "Sure. Albino apes. They're highly prized by the Siamese nobles. They buy 'em up from all over Asia. Like Chinese collect jade, or Frenchmen collect pretty women."

The girl said hastily: "Father, I was telling Mr. McNally about your photography. Maybe he can give you some hints what to look for."

Gatrun was a good man. He was an adventurer of some sort, but—obviously—a capable one. His anger disappeared, as though he had swallowed it; disappeared like the pearls that were much too valuable for an expeditionary photographer's daughter to wear. Mr. Gatrun, it was apparent, could be what he had to be to get along, and for some reason he felt that he ought to be polite to McNally. "I'm most interested in temples," he said. "The Siamese are a sort of Buddhists."

"A very interesting sort," McNally said. "They consider themselves the protectors of Buddhism. The—well, the head guys of it, as it were. Of course, the Thibetans and Chinese and so on pay no attention to all that."

"Very intriguing," Gatrun said. Some sort of signal had passed between him and the girl. "I must talk to you some more." He bowed and took his two hundred pounds back to the drinkers.

The girl rested a hand on McNally's arm. "It's wonderful meeting you," she said. "Father goes to such out of the way places; usually there aren't any nice men at all." She put a little pressure on the hand, swung her head over till it nearly rested on McNally's arm.

Not very subtle, but pleasant. What did they expect to get out of him? A souvenir ape? Well, take them as they come. The sun was warm, the deckchair comfortable, and the scenery interesting. Throw in a pretty girl, and what more could a man ask?

McNally clapped his hands. "A couple of Tom Collinses," he told the steward. That was what man could ask for—a drink.

THE GIRL WAS one of a thousand met in his wanderings in search of the theatrically curious; and the man was not the first who had regarded Dave McNally with suspicion. He forgot about the two of them when the boat docked at the little town of Manak, where he was to go inland. The Chinese storekeeper who had thought enough of the singing cats to wire pre-paid to Singapore met him at the dock. "Mr. McNally?" he asked crisply. "I been waitin' fer yuh. You can flop at my house."

McNally grinned. "Seventh Avenue?"

"Eighth," said the Chinaman, signaling to some younger Chinese to get McNally's bags. "I ran a restaurant there. I was born on Mott Street, though."

"You speak a fine brand of English."

"Thanks, pal. Some of these dopy limeys around here say they can't understand me. Now, mister, about the cats. They sing, see? They don't yowl, they don't squawl, they sing. How's about five grand for them, free and clear?"

"Five hundred," McNally said. "If they're up to expectations." He dropped into the Chinese's brand of talk. "Soon's as they warble *Sweet Rosie O'Grady,* I pay off."

"Not enough," Mr. Ling said. "Good grief, mister, I gotta cut in my cousin what spotted them. And we gotta shell out to the mayor of the town, and a couple district cops, and—"

"How about the man that trained them?" McNally asked. "The owner?"

"A five spot'll cover him," Ling said, offhand.

"Did that restaurant you ran ever sell food?" McNally asked.

"Sure, pretzels and hard-boiled eggs," Ling said. "I quit when repeal come in, and come out here. This was my uncle's joint, he was getting old and wanted to sell out."

They were moving inland, up a flat street. Mud huts and beautifully lacquered teakwood shrines were the local edifices.

"The guy's got the cats," Ling said, "has to go up for his three months. He wants to sell out quick, so's he can buy himself off. Yuh know?"

McNally knew. Most of the citizens of Siam are compelled to work three months a year for the government; a man can buy himself out of it and spend his three months the way he spends the other nine, doing nothing, or, possibly, exerting himself to the extent of training four cats to sing in unison. A good, Siamese activity.

The little people they passed grinned at them cheerfully, amused at the sight of the tall American.

"Of course," McNally said, "I could just give one of these natives a quarter to tell me where the cats are. And buy them without giving you a cent."

"Yeah," Ling said. "Sure. Only, pal, you won't. It would

ruin your racket. You gotta keep up your rep in the sticks around here for being a square shooter. Otherwise, you'd never tumble to a single freak, from one end of the year to the next. Right?"

"I guess so. You're a smart guy, Mr. Ling."

"I get around." They stopped at a concrete-and-tile house, and Ling said: "This is the joint." One side of it was a big store, the rest living quarters. "I wouldn't of wired you, unless I was sure you wouldn't give me the old two X. Like Dutch Schultz, in the old days. If he said he was gonna put you on the spot, he put you. If he said he was gonna slip yuh five grand, at least you got three."

McNally laughed, stepping into the cool house after the hot, dusty street. "You tickle me. If I shut my eyes, I'd think I was back in New York."

A very pretty Siamese girl came out from the store. Ling said something to her in Siamese, and she went away. "Drinks comin' up," Ling said. "How'd ya like the skirt?"

"Very pretty."

"I got five of 'em. I'm the big shot in this town. The only guy here with any ambition."

IT OCCURRED TO McNally that this Ling was as bad an egg as he had met in the Orient. It was going to be a little difficult, doing business with him. Also—well, the singing cat story was a little fishy. Not to McNally, who lived on such fishiness, but— Certainly, Ling was not above inventing a story like that to get a man up here to rob.

McNally said: "Of course, I'd have to pay you in a draft on Singapore. I haven't any cash with me, except for tips."

"That's okay, pal. You got a good name in these parts...." Here's the drinks." He handed McNally a scotch and soda that the girl had brought in, took one himself. "Now, these cats are a half day's drive from here. We—" He broke off to spit angry Siamese at the girl, who was standing there waiting.

She answered him, meekly, and Ling's eyes shot suspiciously to McNally. Then he shrugged. "She says there's a kid in the store askin' if this is where the American's staying. Got a note for you."

"I told one of my agents to spread the word I'd buy albino apes," McNally said, casually. "Here," he gave the girl a coin for the messenger.

Ling said: "Sure, yuh might as well do some side business while you're here." The suspicion left his face, and he nodded to the girl. "I forgot I was dealing with a gent. You wouldn't cross me, would you, pal? Say, I sure miss the old city. Boy, we had some hot times in New York. One night me and some other boys drove over to Brooklyn...."

The girl had come back with the note. She bowed and gave it to McNally, surreptitiously inspecting him at the same time. He took the envelope and opened it. It said:

> *Dear Mr. Gatrun:*
>
> *We welcome you to Siam. There need be no delay if you meet me by the temple of Shiva at nine tonight.*

It was unsigned. McNally whistled. Then he said: "This isn't for me. It's for that fat man—I didn't know he was getting off the boat here.... Got an envelope, Ling?"

Ling nodded, his face icy, suspicious. Nice fellow, Ling, and this was a nice complication. This Chinese would do anything for money, and anything to anybody who stood between him and money. But Ling sent the girl for an envelope.

McNally sealed the letter up again; the original envelope had been unaddressed. He fished up another native coin, tossed it, and put it back in his pocket again. Better to let the messenger wait for his reward till he delivered the note to the right man. "Tell the girl to tell the runner," he said, "that I am the wrong American. I do not know where the other one is staying, but he is the fat American; I am the thin one. If the fat one finds out I read his note, he will beat the runner, otherwise, he will give him money."

"I gotcha," Ling said. He passed the message along to the girl. "When you talk like that, you sound like one of these limeys down in the F.M.S."

"Traveling around, you meet a lot of Englishmen," McNally said, casually.

Ling said: "Yeah. We don't get many up here; the French are the ones who push Siam around…. Now, we'll go see the cats tomorrow; you and me. I'll act as interpreter; I speak the lingo fine. No need you putting out cash for a talker."

"I wasn't going to," McNally said. "I'm in your hands."

"Yeah, you are, Mr. McNally. We'll get along fine. Here—I'll show you to your room; dinner's in an hour. Want another drink, first?"

"I'll wash up, and then we'll have one together."

"Sure, sure," Ling said. "This way. Yeah, we'll make out fine together, Mac. You're in my hands, huh? That's a hot one."

2

THE ROOM WAS cool, expensively furnished in bad taste. He had been a sap, McNally told himself, to come up here this way, in answer to an unknown called Sam Ling. But answering calls like these had gotten him some fancy acts; he had gotten more stuff by accidents of this sort than by any expedition planned in New York or San Francisco. He didn't have more than a few dollars with him in cash, and he had never heard of a Siamese kidnaping.

Outside his room, as he finished washing and lay down on the bed, he could hear singing. The Siamese music was not pretty, though that one girl had a bell-like quality to her voice that was fetching. He got off the bed, stretched, and went to the window.

The girl who had waited on them—evidently Ling's favorite "skirt"—was picking vegetables in a little garden patch. On the kitchen doorstep behind her two other girls, were chopping stuff, and the three of them were singing some plaintive, wailing native song.

McNally noticed, lighting a cigarette, that the garden, that the soil, was just a thin skin of dirt over water. The furrows between the vegetable beds were glistening with it. A country on a swamp, like the terrain around New Orleans.

He was just turning away from the window, when a car

came over the rise near the house, switched off its motor, and drifted noiselessly down the hill. A funny way to arrive, McNally thought, but he didn't think about it hard. Still puffing on his cigarette, his mind was divided between that and wondering whether those rises were natural or artificial....

The car stopped, and the three girls in the kitchen garden stiffened. The pretty one dropped her vegetable basket and went out to the road.

The head that stuck out of the car was male and Chinese, but not purebred Chinese—half Siamese, or Malaysian.... The girl had surreptitiously reached up and touched the face with a gesture at once affectionate and wistful.

The tough Mr. Ling, evidently, was not the lady's man he thought himself. His favorite "skirt's" heart was elsewhere.

One of the girls in the doorway whistled, softly, and the two by the car separated. When Mr. Ling came out the back door of his prosperous house, his girl was picking vegetables again, his visitor was getting out of the car, as though he had just arrived.

The pretty girl's back was to McNally, but the other two were as impassive as bronze Buddhas.

Ling called, softly: "You dope, I told ya not to get here till dark."

The other man took off his felt hat, wiped his face. A white scar ran from one ear down over his nose to the corner of his mouth. He answered something in Chinese.

Ling's hand dropped to his belt, and his yellow face darkened. Then they both turned loose at once, in what McNally could just recognize as Cantonese. McNally could talk a little Chinese, but he couldn't understand the two experts raging at each other in the difficult dialect of Canton.

Ling's hand came away from the gun, and he shrugged. Scarface grinned, the white line twisting the smile into something nasty, and then stepped back into the car, started it, went away, without looking again at either Ling or the girl.

Ling waited a moment, then went back into the house. The girl turned around when one of her two friends said something, and her face was bright with tears….

McNally was lying on his bed thirty seconds later when Ling rapped on the door.

No use admitting he had seen what went on. Ling would have an explanation for it. McNally looked up at his host and yawned. "Pardon me. I've been asleep. Dinner ready?"

"No, not yet. Only, I got lonesome. I don't often see a white guy," said the Chinese. "These natives are a lot of dopes. C'mon down and have another drink."

McNally nodded, and went downstairs. This time, in answer to Ling's clap, one of the other girls brought whisky; McNally guessed that the pretty one was drying out from her cry….

LING AVOIDED MCNALLY'S questions about the cats until after dinner; then he said: "Well, look. It's my cousin that's got them. He's half Siamese, see, my uncle was here for years 'n' years."

"What's wrong with that?" McNally asked. It was seven o'clock; at nine Gatrun was going to meet someone at the temple of Shiva. Shiva, according to McNally's somewhat fragmentary Eastern mythology, was the god of slaughter.

"Well, I thought, now, I was going to take a commission

from each of you. Y'know, let you think I was bein' your agent, let him think I was workin' just fer him. But you're a good guy, McNally. I wouldn't do yuh thataway."

"Nice of you, Ling. No harm done. Just because you've been frank, I'll go to a thousand, if they can really sing."

"One grand, he says. Mex or American?"

"Mex."

"Make it American," said the amazing Mr. Ling, "and it's a deal."

McNally started. Dirty work, dirty, dirty work. This was no boy to cut his price without an argument. Unless the cats were phonies, a ventriloquist act or—But no—Ling was too smart to try anything like that. Because there was nothing else to say, McNally said: "If they really sing."

"They'll sing all right. They'll sing like a bunch of hopheads in the Tombs. Drink?"

"Not me. I can't hold it like you can."

Ling was pleased. "I'm a tough guy. When I was in New York, there was some feeling about me, on accounta I'm Chink. They got over that. Frankie Yale useta say, I was the only Chink in the world could shoot a Tommy with his eyes open. Yeah, I'm tough. One time, me and some of the boys, was sittin' around my place, drinkin' red ink, and I says: 'Let's go over to Brooklyn and....'"

His high, slightly whining voice droned on, recounting old drinking feats, old homicides, old lecheries. A lovely character....

McNally turned over the pieces of jigsaw puzzle that made his situation. The scar-faced man was the cousin who now had the cats and he had not had the cats when Ling wired. That seemed evident, because of the thinness of Sam Ling's story—he was telling McNally because he liked him. The rat never liked anyone in his life.

Had the cousin killed the owner of the cats? Possibly, but this was a peaceful sort of country; homicide was likely to be noticed. Besides which, any Siamese would have sold the animals for fifty dollars. And Ling was too cautious a man to make a murder for that small a sum.

Okay, then. The expeditionary photographer, whose daughter wore a five thousand dollar string of pearls. How about him? Why had he gotten off the boat in this little village? The pictures would be in the capital, farther up the river. And why was he meeting someone at the temple of Shiva after dark…?

Looking out the window, fog was blanketing Siam like a cloak. Nobody went out after dark. Nobody but….

McNally took another drink.

He would get himself obviously plastered, and insist on going for a walk. He could find the temple of Shiva. The town was small, Shiva unmistakeable.

One of the girls entered and waited for Ling to notice her. When he did, she delivered a message.

The ex-gangster laughed, and slapped his knee. "A twist to see ya, Mac. A white twist, according to Prika here. Boy, you must have somethin' to have 'em foller yuh up the river to this dump."

"It must be that other American's daughter," McNally said, smiling thinly. Yes, he had been right. Gatrun, was somehow, messed up in this mystery.

Ling had already sent the girl away. She came back, stood aside, and Lisa Gatrun came in. "Hello," she said gaily. "Am I interrupting anything? Dad got talking to a couple of priests about temples, and I was so bored I hired a boy to find you."

"Swell to see you," McNally said. "My host, Mr. Ling, Miss Gatrun."

"Welcome to our nest," said Ling. "Have a drink. Have a couple of 'em."

"With pleasure," Lisa said. She took the chair next to McNally, put her hand on his arm in the same gesture she had used on the boat after her father had signaled to her.

That signal, it was now apparent, meant: "Work on the sucker." McNally told himself he had fallen among thieves, and tough ones, too. He had minded Ling, because he could not get at Ling's motives; he minded the girl more. A girl so pretty, so sweet, to be a crook was somehow horrible; and McNally was a tough man, tough in a way that put Ling's cheap murdering to shame.

THEY TALKED ABOUT New York, and the clock rolled on; it was eight and after when McNally said: "By the way, the Maharajah of one of the states in India commissioned me to get him an idol while I was here. A Shiva. Know of any good ones?"

Ling was excited by the girl, careless, hardly listening. For the past half hour he had been nearly rude to McNally.

"There's a temple of Shiva just past here, along the bank. I dunno if it's any good.... Tell me, Miss Gatrun, you ever drink a eleven-ring pousse café? When I had my restaurant on Eight Avenue...."

McNally watched the clock, watched the girl, watched Ling. The girl's charm was kneading McNally's biceps quietly, unnoticeably; she was a good obedient daughter, no doubt. *Work on the sucker.*

Hot, white anger filled McNally. To be taken for a simpleton by a bunch of petty-larceny crooks like this was too much! The girl with her obvious blandishments, Ling with his cheap business tricks....

McNally said: "Look, Lisa, I'm going to take you home. Ling and I have work tomorrow."

Ling forgot himself. He snarled: "Let the dame talk for herself. She knows when—" Then he remembered. Some business dealing depending on McNally. "Okay. Tomorrow's another night. Come for chow, Miss Gatrun?"

"I'll be gone by then," McNally said. "I hope. We'll See the cats by noon, you say?"

"Yeah, we'll see the cats." Ling didn't look at him. "C'mon fer dinner, and bring your old man, if you want to."

"I'll see what his plans are, and send you a note in the morning," the girl said, smiling. She stood up, took McNally's arm; they went outside, McNally saying: "Don't wait up for me, Ling. Just so I can get in."

"I never lock the joint. Nobody around here'd rob Sam Ling," the Chinese boasted.

McNally grinned and took Lisa Gatrun out into the damp, foggy night. The heat of the day had been trapped and moistened by the mist; it was stifling out, after the cool house.

"We'll go by the ridge," McNally said. "It'll be drier."

"But we're staying just a little ways down...."

He put his hard arm around her waist, pulled her to him. He made his voice a little drunken, a little amorous. "There'll be a moon up on the bank—Lisa."

She said: "All right!" Her voice was high, nervous, and he wondered if he had misjudged her. She did not seem to be accustomed to the devious game her father had set her playing.

They climbed the ridge, holding each other by the hand. In the fog, a man couldn't see ten feet.

He stopped when they came into the moonlight, put a hand on her shoulder, turned her toward him. As his arms went around her, he could see his wrist watch. Quarter of nine. He tilted her chin up.

"No. Please, no—Dave. I'm scared."

Maybe this was a game. He said: "You're sweet, Lisa. I like you."

She caught his hand in her two, swung away from him. "I like you, too, Dave. I do, really I do. But don't kiss me, now. I can't tell you why. Just—just take me back to where we're staying, and go back to Ling's."

"I want to walk along the bank."

The girl was nearly crying. "Don't! Don't! I—I'll go back down the river with you tomorrow. I'll do it, really I will. Only go back to Ling's."

Maybe this wasn't acting. It had a sincere ring to it. McNally said: "I want to have a look at that temple of Shiva Ling was talking about."

"Oh—you fool!" she cried. "Men! Money and men and men and money and—"

He touched the pearls at her throat. "Marbles don't buy those."

Her hand stung along his cheek for a moment, and she turned, stumbling, then ran away, down below again, into the pool of mist that was the town. McNally ran after her, but he lost her in the fog; when he finally heard her high heels clicking on stone in the distance the sound was immediately followed by a door slamming.

He turned back, looked at his watch. Ten minutes to nine. He took his .38 automatic out of his hip pocket, pumped a shell from the clip into the chamber, and went back up the hill to the ridge.

At two minutes of nine, a huge, monstrous idol of the god of slaughter loomed out of the fog, and he was at the temple of Shiva.

A STONE OR a shell rolled and went clashing away. White tendrils of fog drifted up from below in a soft, hot wind that had sprung up. McNally called: "It is nine o'clock."

A voice sibilant, oriental, said: "Gatrun?"

McNally said: "Yes!"

Then his white hat was gone from his head, and a chip of stone was gone from Shiva's base. The fog drifting up distorted all human life, all emotions, and it seemed to McNally that the bullet had clipped into his hat before he heard the shot.

He dropped to the ground and waited. The fog collected around Shiva's base and stayed there, while the moonlight shone on the indescribably ugly face of the sinister God of Slaughter above McNally's head.

After a while the same voice called: "I think they've gone now. Come here."

They must take Gatrun for an awful fool. Dave McNally lay still.

He lay there two minutes, maybe three, but it didn't seem that long. Sometimes when you are scared, time stands still, and other times you are so scared that you would willingly lie hidden for years and think them a moment. So thought

Dave McNally, while the damp ground of the ridge chilled him, and the hot air of Siam made him sweat, and fear held him still as the ugly leering god so near him.

A horrid, reddening groan split the night. "Gatrun. Ohhhhhh, Gatrun, they've shot me!"

McNally added teeth chattering to his other uncomfortable activities, and tried to lie still. But that groaning went on.

"Come, come here, Gatrun, I'm dying." And then: "Quick, so I can tell you—"

And then Gatrun's voice, Gatrun erect, Gatrun just arriving. "Key? Are you there, Key?"

Another shot. Dave McNally fired at the flash, squeezed the trigger of his automatic twice, and made a quick run forward, towards the man who had shot at both him and Gatrun.

The strange gun roared again. But it wasn't firing at McNally but at Gatrun. The heavy man screamed and McNally turned.

Such was the trickery of the fog that Gatrun seemed to end at the waist. His shoulders and head and chest were as visible as they had been on the boat; his lower half was gone, bathed in fog.

Somebody had scrawled across his face in black ink, shiny black ink. While McNally watched him, transfixed, the invisible hand extended that black ink further, till it hit the big man's collar; Gatrun was wounded in the head, and fumbling for a gun. The third man, whoever he was, ended the business right then; his bullet nearly took Gatrun's chest away.

Gatrun had gotten his gun out just before then; his

dying anguish squeezed the trigger, and bullets cut dirt out of the floor of Shiva's temple yard.

McNally really ran now, ran bent over, hiding under the fog, his hand hard on his gun, his fear replaced by unreasoning anger. Ahead of him, someone stumbled into a stone, and McNally snapped a cap at the noise; but then a motor roared, and a car got out of there without lights.

McNally pulled up, panting hard, feeling spent and useless in the night. No use chasing a car on foot through this foggy, dank night; he struck a match, peered around. Small feet—men's feet in sandals, but small ones—had made holes in the temple ground, and there was a trail that looked like blood.

Maybe it was Shiva's influence but McNally was glad, happy, fiercely proud that he had at least wounded the man.

Then he thought of Gatrun and went back, fumbling and stumbling among the shards and rubble of the temple yard. He nearly stepped on the big man's outstretched hand before he found him.

When McNally struck a match and bent down, he knew there was nothing more to be done there. Lisa's father was dead. You didn't have to touch him, or even look very closely to know that.

McNally thought of his own footprints in that damp temple yard. Thought of them too late. There were to many to be covered, and they were unmistakably his in that country of tiny folk.

He got out of there, too, not at all happy. This was what came of mixing into things before they mixed into you. He should have gone to bed like a good little boy, and met tomorrow's troubles as they came up, instead of trying to solve them by moonlight and fog.

3

MCNALLY DID WHAT few men could have done under the circumstances; he went to bed. Not only to bed, but to sleep.

True, he crumpled paper—two old copies of *Variety*—around his bed as an alarm clock for marauders; but he slept. There was an underlying hardness in him that was necessary to his business. When he had something he thought he ought to do, he did it; but tonight there was nothing. Almost as an afterthought he cleaned the shoes he had worn and pulled the heel off one of them; tomorrow he would wear his other pair of white shoes, almost identical as to uppers, but leather soles instead of rubber. It was all that could be done to confuse any investigation that might ensue.

Another man would have found Lisa Gatrun and told her her father was dead. Dave McNally had carried worse messages to prettier girls; he was not afraid of the unpleasant chore. But there was no use causing the girl to lose a night's sleep; nothing could now be done for her father.

A less experienced man might have packed and tried to make it out of the country. But there are no borders in the Orient for the white man who has been mixed up in a killing. French, English and the rest of Europe's traditional enemies unite when they get East of Suez to promote the fiction of the white man's supremacy; it goes hard with the man who jeopardizes that commercial commodity.

So McNally went to sleep, and dreamed, curiously enough, of being back with the circus as press agent.

He awoke at six; the crumpled newspaper was rustling. His hand went under his pillow, his fingers closed on the gun.

Then he rolled, pulling the automatic under the covers and sitting up all at once. Dawn was making the windows pink; dawn was putting an unhealthy glow on Sam Ling's yellow face.

Ling said: "Light sleeper, ain't you? Get up, we're rolling."

Had there, or had there not been a knife in Ling's hand just before McNally's eyes were completely open? Hard to tell, now. Something had shone.

McNally docilely got up. "Be down in a minute." As Ling started for the door, McNally called: "By the way, how far did you say these cats were?"

"Ten miles."

"Okay."

Ten miles in a car, over the worst roads or no roads at all, shouldn't take them more than an hour each way. It was now six. They should be back by ten. If the cousin wanted to bargain, let him come back in the car with them. McNally would be needed by the girl.

To have your father die is bad. To have him die up the river in Siam is a great deal worse. No friends, no home, nothing— Well, she had McNally. But McNally was a business man. Cats came first—four singing cats.

Downstairs, two of the girls had breakfast ready—coffee,

tea, curry, toast. McNally ate absent-mindedly. With his mouth full of toast, he said: "Guess I got pretty gay last night."

Ling was still his hard, day self. "I mix a good drink, how'd you make out with the twist?" He winked, nastily.

McNally returned the wink, his being revolted by this man. "Okay."

"Yeah?" Ling laughed. "You was back by five minutes of nine. I heard ya."

Dave McNally choked on a piece of food. He didn't like mysteries, had no use for them; and this was making a nasty one. He had not been back at half past nine, and Ling knew it; therefore Ling had reason, and that reason could only be that he wanted to alibi McNally on the temple of Shiva business.

The mystery cleared up, in part. "This cat deal is a pretty piece of change," Sam Ling said. "I'd hate for it to fall through for any reason."

"Yeah," McNally said drily, "such as me falling into jail."

"Since you put a name on it," the Chinese said, "yeah. You stick to business till you get outa Siam. I got influence here, and I can cover yah on this Gatrun mess. Why'd you croak the old boy?"

"I didn't," McNally said.

"Sure you didn't," Ling laughed, pushing back from the table, wiping crumbs off his mouth. "Sure. Anybody's buying five grand worth of cats from the Ling family couldn't do nothing—not in Siam. But from now on, you stay close to the house. All the profit'll go out of this soon."

"The price was a thousand yesterday," McNally said.

"That was yesterday. This is today, the morning after last night. Let's roll."

THEY WENT OUTSIDE to the courtyard; there was a car there. It was the same aged convertible that the scar-faced Chinese had driven yesterday. The Ling family bus, evidently. One of the girls brought them a bottle of whisky, and Ling started the motor, inexpertly.

They bumped out of the courtyard and onto the road that made a sharp little twist and gained its way up to the top of the embankment. They bumped along the ridge to the temple of Shiva; a group of chattering Siamese were running around the temple yard, grinning and calling to each other. Like rubbernecks in front of a house where a body has been found.

A cop in the road saluted Sam Ling with gravity and deference. Yes, Dave McNally would be all right, so long as he played things Ling's way.

He cursed himself for being nosy the night before. It had cost him four thousand dollars. There were times to bargain, and times not to, and Ling had him as tight as ever a racketeer had a speakeasy proprietor in the old days in New York, the days that had taught Ling his methods.

A nasty thought crossed McNally's mind. Supposing the cats couldn't sing? Supposing they were just four ordinary Siamese cats—worth fifty to a couple of hundred dollars set down in New York—and the whole plan had been Ling's own species of blackmail. Yeah, supposing that. And he, Dave McNally, had fallen for it.

They passed groups of men, doing their compulsory labor by working on the embankment. They bumped on, and in half an hour, they were at a halt in the courtyard of a mud house, a little larger than the ordinary, but no mansion like Sam Ling's.

There had been plenty of time the night before, to make it out here to see the cats. Sam Ling had planned this thing, one way or another, and McNally was caught.

They got out of the car, and the door of the house opened. A lean man—taller than any Siamese—came out, tugging at his battered felt hat. When he got it off, it was the scar-faced half-breed who was in love with Ling's favorite wife.

Ling said: "Mr. McNally, this is my cousin, Ling Key."

Key said, stumblingly: "Pleesta-meetcha."

"It's a pleasure," McNally drawled. "You have the cats?"

"Velly fline cats, misteh. You like 'em."

"Sure, I'll take 'em if they can sing. Fetch 'em out."

"You clome in here, please."

Sam Ling had been silent through all this, his thin lips twisted up into a little strange smile. He nodded, and he and McNally went into the house.

The cats were not caged. They came surging forward friendlily, anxious to greet the company. They were handsome beasts, big Siamese with seal-brown ears and tails and legs, beige bodies. One of them wrapped himself around McNally's ankles, and the American bent over, patted her. She said: "Mrrreouwww," with the peculiar sharp inflection Siamese cats have.

"You see," Key said.

He stepped to a xylophone, marimba, or whatever they were called in Siam. With a felt-covered mallet he softly struck a note; the four cats left off being a greeting committee, and leaped for a stand behind the instrument.

Nice flash, there, McNally thought. One of the males

had gone right across the board of the xylophone without touching it, his body a tan, quick arc in the air. Yeah, that'd look good behind the footlights.

"Tune 'em up, Key," Sam Ling said. He dropped into a chair, lit a cigarette. "This is the part I like best, Mac."

Ling Key strung a bar in front of the first cat; the cat sounded off in a low, almost bass voice that flatted the bar. Key tried it again, and on the third try, the cat caught the note matched it.

In turn he tuned up each cat till he had it matched with the instrument, all the cats on the middle C's of their voices. Then he let go.

The tune he played was a native one, hardly music to Occidental ears, but still, unmistakably a tune. The cats kept time and tone with the xylophone.

KEY FINISHED WITH a flourish, holding his mallet off the bars and conducting with his free hand while the cats repeated the theme of the song. Then he hit a chord with mallet and hand, and turned, bowing.

"Give 'em *Sing Something Simple*," Ling said. "This was my idea, Mac. They oughta have a song the customers can catch."

Key bowed, and held up his free hand for the cats to watch. In quick time they ran through the little revue number of eight years ago; and again they finished even and true.

"Okay," Ling said. "Is it an act?"

"It's an act," McNally said. His problem was a little simpler now. He at least knew that he wanted to buy the cats. "How will they work for a stranger?"

"With a couple of weeks rehearsal," Ling said, "Okay. Key can teach you on the boat."

"Key? Does he go with me?"

"Yeah," Sam Ling said. "Key goes with you. Otherwise, no deal. Anyway, the cats wouldn't be no use to ya without him. He can teach you, and you can teach whoever you put in charge of the act. Key'll drop off at Suez."

McNally stretched his legs. "And what," he asked, "does Key smuggle out with him?"

"You can have the act for four grand," Ling said. "I like you, Mac. Four grand."

"A thousand," McNally said. Might as well bluff it out. The cats, through with their act, were prowling around the room, making friends. Key went out and came back with a plate of fish, which he divided equally among his performers. They growled and snapped happily as they gulped it.

"A thousand, and Key takes no baggage with him," McNally said.

He kept his eyes on Ling.

Ling dropped his hands to his felt waistband and stood up. "Don't get tough, Mac," he said. "You can take in a grand a week from them cats in the vaudeville swing."

"Vaudeville's dead," McNally said. "I'll have to get them a spot in a fair someplace. And Siamese cats don't travel well; they get pneumonia. One grand."

Ling took his gun part way out of his belt. "Make it rough for me," he said. "G'wan, make it hard. We was doing business like gents when you have to get like this," he complained.

"I can play any xylophone a little," McNally said. "I'll pick up the act quickly. I don't need Key."

"You can't play any xylophone in the hoosegow," said Ling. "Now, you made me say it. That Gatrun caught you with his daughter up in the temple yard, and you croaked him. Nice guy."

"Oh, no," McNally said. He had reached a decision. "Key here killed him. He was arranging with that wife of yours—you know, the pretty one—to get out of the country as Gatrun's servant. You discovered them and—"

Key's English was not good, but it covered anything this close to home. He shrieked: "Liar!" at McNally and two yards of Chinese at Ling.

McNally hated to do it, but he waited till the storm subsided, said: "I happened to be looking out the window yesterday. He drifted the car down to your courtyard, made love to your wife till you came out. Then he acted just as though he had just gotten there."

Ling said: "We got Torpedo Marrone's gang that way. Gettin' 'em to fight against each other, broke 'em up. It don't go, McNally. You was in that templeyard, and the cops know it, and I own the cops."

McNally laughed. "Okay. Whatever it is, you must want it out of the country awfully bad to see your prettiest wife go with it."

Sam Ling stood there, his thin face puzzled, his eyes cloudy. He looked from one man to the other, muttering tough sentences that meant nothing. "No guy double-crossses me.... I ain't no one to fool with.... Youse guys oughta be scared of me...." But it got him no place. He could fight, but he wasn't a very quick thinker.

Suddenly he stopped: "Put them cats in their cage, and come on. We'll argue this at my joint."

He acted as though he couldn't bear to be away from the suspected wife another moment. Maybe it was love, maybe it was just that he had to go on believing he was tops. A guy that couldn't hold a twist was a punk.

4

THE CATS HOPPED into their crate happily; apparently they were cats who enjoyed traveling. Ling and McNally got in front, and Key got next to his crate. They started off.

The houses in this town, as in Ling's were all below the embankment. Maybe that was government property, though it seemed silly. Maybe living on it broke it down. It was obviously built for flood control, to hold the river waters away from the towns.

They started climbing up to the top, and a ragged native, blood-stained and gravel scarred, rushed out and made a speech. Ling kicked down hard on the gas.

"Fakir," he said. "Phony religious guy. There's lots of 'em around here."

"Yes?" The man hadn't looked like any fakir McNally had ever seen in a Buddhist country. Buddhists—especially lower-class ones—often went in for a second, more workaday religion, but seldom for such a dirty one. Well, add it to the rest of the troubles.

They bumped along the embankment. A noble's house that they passed had an albino ape in a big bamboo cage in front. McNally said: "If I make a good deal with you, can you get me a couple of those white apes?"

Ling said: "I don't keep no bird shop. Five grand for the cats and Key goes along. I ain't bargaining."

His voice was nasty.

McNally shrugged. It was time to keep his mouth shut. He had thrown one little seed of discord into the Key-Ling combination, and it might come to something. A man couldn't tell. If you went into this business determined never to act without a plan, you ended up sitting on a dock on the North River. Act first and think it out afterwards and play them as they come.

Ling was using the bottle his wife had given him.

They bumped into Key's courtyard, and the prettiest wife came out to greet them. Ling growled at her in Siamese as he got out of the car; his feet missed and he stumbled. He had nearly emptied the bottle.

She wailed in answer, and cried something that made Ling laugh without good humor. He turned. She says: 'Not even a worm could love the scar-faced one!' You lied, Mac, and I'm goin' to—"

Key's eyes were anxious as he said: "Pahdon my clousin, Mr. McNally. Him drunk." He added Chinese words that made Ling stop scowling drunkenly at Key.

"Okay," Ling said. "We need ya, McNally. You won't cross us up; you're too smart." He staggered toward the house, leaning on the wife. Another of his girls came to get him.

McNally said: "Quick, Key. We have the car. Get the girl, and we'll make it down the river."

"No savvy."

"You savvy plenty," McNally cried. He stiff-armed the man and ran. This was a sucker move, this was dumb, but there had been a little worry gnawing at him for a long time. He took the car through the town, twisting and turning, trying to find the house the girl had slammed into in the dark the night before.

He could make little more than a snail's pace in the narrow, turning alleys. Looking in the mirror, he saw Key running along behind. Well, maybe the half breed wanted his cats back. McNally wished he had never heard of the singing cats.

Here, this must be the house. It was the quarter she had held to, and the largest house in the neighborhood. But if he went in, Key would get the car and the cats.

McNally fumbled in his pocket as he climbed out of the car. A crowd clustered around the American, chattering and laughing. His hand came up filled with coins, and he opened it, scattering them wide all around the car.

The natives instantly went down on their hands and knees, looking for the pennies from heaven. Let Key get out of there in less than five minutes!

McNally dashed at the house, tried the door. It was open. He tore in, shouting: "Lisa! Lisa!"

The girl appeared from the next room. She had on a white linen dress, and her face was nearly as white as the cloth. He shouted: "Come on, I've got a car. They killed your father and they're going to kill—"

A voice behind him spat something in the native tongue, and he turned, jerking out his gun. Then he lowered the muzzle, and stood, quietly; there were a half dozen police in the door, diminutive in their shorts and khaki shirts and belts, but armed. It was their leader, a sergeant who had spoken.

Lisa sobbed: "He's the one, he's the one. He—he

followed us up on the boat," and then collapsed, weeping on the arm of a chair.

The sergeant produced a pair of American handcuffs, huge in his tiny brown hands, and said, *"Merci."*

McNally asked in French: "What is the charge against me?"

The sergeant shrugged, said something in Siamese. Evidently: "Thanks" was all the French he knew. And no English.

TWO OF THE little cops threatened McNally with their guns, and the American put his hands out. The sergeant clasped the bracelets on, said something to one of his men. The man stepped forward, bowed to Lisa. "Sergeant say, you rike us keep this man by jail?"

"Yes," the girl said. She was very tall, almost stately. "He killed my father. You are to hold him until we get his record from the United States."

The cop translated this for the sergeant, who asked a short question. "Sergeant say," the translator said, "him gangster?"

The girl said: "Yes. A New York gangster. Ling sent for him."

"Rike in pictures?" asked the cop.

The girl nodded. The cop said something, and all the cops looked at McNally with interest. One of them muttered. "Okay. Le'm have rit," and they all grinned, proudly. Evidently they were patrons of the cinema.

But McNally was not amused. He said to the girl: "What nonsense is this? I have no record in the States. I'm a business man, my agent is Jake Loeb in the Bond Building, New York, and—"

The girl said: "Oh, stop it. You killed my father. Maybe you can beat the trial, maybe you can intimidate—"

McNally said: "Wait a minute. Hold on. I've been dumb. This Ling I've been staying with—he's been pulling gangster stuff around here? Running a racket?"

"Yes," she said. "You know it. He sent for you to help him. Because my father—"

McNally said: "Your father was a private detective. Okay, I got it, now. Listen, tell this monkey to take my handcuffs off so I can think. I'll—"

She said: "Forget it. Father's dead, but the job he came here to do isn't over. He—"

"Shut up, woman!" McNally barked. "My papers are inside my coat here. Take them out, look at them. Press clippings of me landing with animals, photographs."

The girl moved forward, timidly, got the papers out of a big seal wallet, opened them. "Oh," she said. "Oh. You—you were telling the truth, Dave."

He said: "Tell this monkey to take my bracelets off. We gotta hurry, we—"

The girl gave an order to the interpreter, the interpreter passed it along, and McNally was free.

"Him not gangster?" asked the interpreter. Nobody answered him.

McNally was thinking hard. "Ling got me up here to help him get something out of the country. The English are so used to me they'd let me into the F.M.S. without examination…. The spoils, I suppose. He was ready for the clean-up. Then he heard your father was coming. And then…."

The front door had no lock on it, apparently, because it

opened as easy for Sam Ling as it had for the cops. Ling said: "Okay, McNally. You'll do fine if you don't see this gal again. Boys, take him back to my place and—"

The sergeant turned a puzzled face, and Ling cried: "Them ain't local cops!" and filled his hand with his gun. The sergeant and one of the cops got their own revolvers out, but the Chinese was gone by then. The heavy door stared blankly at them.

"The Regent sent these police down to help my father," Lisa said. "Ling had bought up all the local ones…. The Regent is a—a legal-minded man. The old rulers would have killed Ling, but he wanted the proof. Wanted to catch him at it. Ling has been hiding behind his cousin, the man they call Ling Key.…"

"That's it," Dave McNally said. "I was to get Ling Key out. Then Ling could put all the blame on him, hide the money. When Key was picked up, he would be accused of having spent the money or hidden it outside the country. Yeah, I got it. This business of Ling's, his legitimate one, is too valuable for him to leave. That man loves a dollar! So he could keep the spoils from the racket, from shaking down everybody in the district, and still go on here legally.…"

"Stop talking!" the girl said. "Do something, Dave. Ling's desperate."

McNally went to the window, looked out. The street was strangely deserted. Key's car still stood there, the cats on the back seat in their crate.

"All right," McNally said. "I'll try." He looked around the room. There was a trapdoor to the flat roof, a ladder. He set it in place, started to climb.

Lisa stepped forward, stopped.

The interpreter and the sergeant chattered. The interpreter said: "Maybe so him G-man?"

"Tell him I'm Harpo Marx," McNally said, and pushed the trap door open, went on the roof.

It was hot up there, hot and sunny, not unpleasant. McNally crept across the roof, because this place was commanded by the embankment, and he was in the range of fire. And Ling would fire. Ling would stay true to type. **FUNNY. MCNALLY SUPPOSED,** as he crawled along the flat roof, that he would be running into traces of American prohibition all over the globe, for years. Repeal had smashed up the gangs, taken their living away, but it had not changed the minds of the men who had composed those gangs. Ling, trying to pull New York rackets in Siam, had done only what other foreign gangsters had done on returning to their native hearths; Europe was honeycombed with little rackets.

There—he was to the edge. He lay flat, only his forehead and eyes over the edge of the roof, and peered around. They were not on the embankment, as he had expected; they were in a shrine across the street. They would have their eyes on the front door.

McNally swung himself down to the top of the car, nearly bounced off the tight canvas, grabbed the edge and rolled. His hand closed on the heavy cat cage, and he caught it, loped for the door, and was behind the heavy teak when the first bullet roared.

"Made it," he gasped. "It's all right." The girl stared at the cats. "All right? I thought you were going to get us out of here?"

McNally said: "Huh? And leave the cats? Say, this is the best act I've seen in months. It's—"

"If all you wanted was to get those cats inside the house," the girl said, "why didn't you just go and get them?"

"They'd be watching the front door," McNally said. "As soon as it started to open they'd shoot. I had to show up from some other angle, take them by surprise."

He set the cage on the floor.

The girl said: "Well, I hope you and your cats have a nice time. I still don't see how we'll get out of here."

"That'll come," McNally said. He kneeled, reached a finger into the cage. "Nice kitties. Say, I wonder when they eat? I wouldn't want them to get sick."

"Cats!" said the girl, and turned her back.

"Well, they're my living," said McNally. "You wouldn't have a can of salmon around?" He cooed at the cats. Boy, Jake ought to be able to get them a spot in the World's Fair itself. At a quarter admission, they'd show six a day, to a thousand people a time. Six, hell, they'd show— A man'd need an adding machine to figure out how much they'd make.

He'd get a cute little girl pianist, dressed up in tights, They'd perform for anyone if they would for Ling Key, who had surely just stolen them, taken them from their rightful trainer—

A burst of pistol shots broke up his reverie. He turned.

The sergeant and one of his cops were leaning on the sill of one of the little windows, their guns pointed out. It was one of their guns that McNally had heard, but it was not one of theirs that spoke next. A gat across the street boomed, and the cop fell back, clawing at his forehead.

McNally rushed forward, pulled the cop away; he was dead, the bullet had drilled his brain.

Ling had said he was the only Chink who could shoot a Tommy with his eyes open. Yes, he could shoot all right.

McNally pulled the sergeant out of the window, cried: "Wait till dark. I—wait till dark, anyway, we'll try and get out the back way." Peering out the window, he could see police uniforms in with Ling, too. Local cops. If the cops from the Regency got them, they would be killed; Siamese law invoked the death penalty easy. So they would be desperately on Ling's side.

The interpreter was frantically telling the sergeant what McNally had said. He finished, waited for a question, turned to the American: "Sergeant say, you G-man?" When McNally nodded, the interpreter grinned: "Hokay, then we wait."

McNally said: "Was your father a G-man, Lisa?"

"No," she said, "he was a bank detective. He came out here to organize the force for a chain of banks in China."

"If he'd been a G-man, he could have ruled this country. Good old Hollywood. I wish we had Jimmy Cagney here, we could scare the opposition to death."

She said: "If you'd stop making jokes and plan something—"

"Oh, leave me alone," McNally said. "I've already figured it out. This is just a mud house. Set your little cops here to scratching at the back wall with their fingernails, and we'll have a hole to crawl through by dark."

"Well, why didn't you say so?"

He waved a hand.

"I'm thinking about cats. You don't suppose it's bad for them to stay in their cage?"

She didn't answer, but went and talked to the interpreter. In a few minutes the cops, armed with table knives, were digging at the back wall.

5

OF ALL THE wild things that had ever happened to McNally, this came close to being tops. Besieged in a house in backwater Siam by gangsters! But for all its idiocy, it was time to make it away from here. The river boat was due at six, and he wanted to be on it; he and his cats. Last night he had worried about the girl, but not since she had turned him in as a gangster.

Yeah, make it to the boat, get down the river, where his influence could be used, and leave the government to fight it out with Ling. He, McNally, had gotten what he came for, and so—farewell.

He sat near his cats and watched the little cops scratch mud out of the back wall. At two he said: "Tell 'em to lay off, Lisa. We don't want to drive a truck through; just get our cage out."

She jumped up.

"The cage! All you think about is those cats."

"Well, that's the widest thing to go. By the way, whose house is this?"

"The district governor's. He was killed a month or so ago. The government—"

"They'll probably send you a bill for destroying their property. Oriental governments are notoriously ungrateful.

Once in India a rajah—one of the little hill rajahs—asked me to kill a tiger that was annoying his—"

"Oh, stop it!" she cried. "If you're talking to cheer me up, stop it! I get so tired of your long-winded reminiscences."

"All right, but that's no way to win friends and influence people."

"I'm engaged to a boy in Pekin."

"I bet he's either a bank clerk or a missionary." McNally got up and went to the front window. There was a possibility that Ling and his gang of crooked cops were gone.

He could see no one moving in the shrine across the way. He stepped closer, got right in front of the window.

Across the street metal glinted, and he threw himself to the floor. The bullet went right through the room and broke a water jug on a table on the opposite wall.

McNally slowly picked himself up off the floor. Ling was not going to let them out of there alive. The Chinese had gone to too much trouble— So much planning. Locating the cats, wiring McNally—building Key up to steal the cats. No, Ling was not going to let them out. Presumably he was going to start a civil war if necessary. Or, more probably, he was counting on the government dropping the whole thing if their squad of police didn't come back.

The girl said: "Had it occurred to you that Ling will know you are trying to make the boat? Just before boat time, he'll probably make sure we're still in here."

"Yeah," McNally said, slowly. "I thought of that. And I thought of something else. If there's a fight on the way to the boat, one of these cats is going to get hurt. So"—he grinned painfully—"if you will persuade one of your little brown friends to give me a couple of guns, I'll go take Mr.

Ling for you now. I don't want to," cried McNally. "I've always been a guy that tended strictly to his own business. None of this damsel-rescuing or law-enforcing for me. But, darn it, they might chase me and hurt a cat if I try and run for it."

The girl looked at him. She spoke to the interpreter, and the interpreter spoke to the sergeant, and two guns were handed over; McNally added them to his own. There would be no time for reloading where he was going.

He went to the hole the little man had dug, and bent over. "Hey," he said, "would you mind putting a dish of water in the cage? They might get thirsty."

"Yes," the girl said. "I'll—I'll do anything for them. Nice cats." Her eyes were bright.

"Hey," McNally said, "I'm not doing this for you. I gotta get my—aw—" He bent over her, kissed her. It did no harm to let her think what she wanted to think. Good for her ego.

The sergeant had been storing up something. He let it rip now. "Hooray for G-men," he said, and beamed.

"Yeah," McNally rasped. "Hooray for the G-men." He slid through the hole in the wall and was out in the sunlight of an alley. His feet squnged through the muck and mud, and he crept along, going parallel to the street. It was not funny that Ling had not surrounded the house; there were no windows in the back of it, and a mud house won't burn. It would take a stranger to think of scratching through the mud; a native would be used to thinking of these walls as solid.

So down the alley, and when you turned into the street, you would be for it. The chances are the cops would have elderly revolvers, and not be very good at using them; rural cops in an Oriental country would not have the same good equipment as the Regency officers.

And if you're going to die now, McNally, it's high good time. You've been in tighter spots than this, and earned a death or so—

MCNALLY WAS AT the first corner of the alley. Of course, he could go on a way, and make a wide circle, and try and sneak up on Ling from the rear. But the shrine was pretty open all the way around.

He turned into the cross alley, made it nearly to the street when he was spotted. A lookout shouted, and a knife flew at him, a silver line through the air.

McNally fired, and ducked, and the knife missed him by inches. Ought to duck faster next time. But the lookout was gone. Down.

McNally sprinted around the corner and ducked into a doorway. A sleek head moved in the shrine, and he fired at it, sure it was Ling's; but he missed, because the Chinese came into view for a moment, his face bright and interested over the barrel of a sub-machine gun. How, McNally wondered as bullets sprayed into the mud around him, did the Chinese mug ever smuggle a Tommy into the country?

Not that it mattered. The Tommy was real enough, and the bullets that were giving smallpox to the mud doorway were real enough. One of them ricocheted off a stone in the wall, and slugged next to McNally's left hand. The flat hunk of lead fell to the damp ground and sizzled.

McNally waited till the burst of fire had ceased, and then took a deep breath and a hard, slow grip on his own automatic and one of the police specials the sergeant had given him. There was nothing to do but step out and snipe. Nothing in the world to do....

It was funny, he was thirsty, terribly thirsty. You wouldn't think a man could think of that now? One step, two steps. He found he was taking tiny little paces, inches long. Because he hated to leave the defilade of the doorway. Defilade. Yeah, he had learned that word during the war. It meant being protected by a little mound, or a doorway, or anything to keep those bullets away.

Defilade. Give me a sentence with the word defilade....

Without the use of his brain, his will power, at all, he had taken himself out of the doorway, was standing in the street, and his hands were squeezing the guns with slow, steady squeezes that sent a bullet every time a target showed in the shrine.

One of the crooked cops with Ling stood up and screeched, then staggered forward into the dirty street, clawing at his throat. The diversion gave McNally a second in which to lose another round, and he thought he got another cop before the Tommy came swiveling at him and he had to duck back into his nice, friendly doorway.

Bad shooting, McNally. Terrible shooting. Six bullets and only two men. He took shells out of one police special and loaded the other one full up. He still had his eight-shot automatic, with five shells in it.

Yes, he still had that, and he had his life, and he had this doorway, but Ling had the Tommy and was using it. Sooner or later that Tommy would knock enough wall away so's it wouldn't cover McNally.

There would be notes in *Variety* and *Billboard: Dave McNally, noted purveyor of sideshow novelties, was killed in a fight in Siam, according to information received. McNally was 38, and had been in show business since 1915, except for war service.*

The graves in Siam are built above ground, because the high water table makes it impossible.

Where had he heard that? *Baedeker,* or an encyclopedia, or was he thinking of another country? It didn't matter, because it was now time to make another sniping expedition, But it seemed a shame that a man's last thought should be one that was quite probably inaccurate.

All right. This is the street, and that warm feeling on your chilly back is sun, and that sleek black thing is Ling's head, so let him have it....

Wop, wop, wop, wop. Boy, you are very, very hot, because you have gotten two more of Ling's little cops, and the China boy is pretty well alone and—

There comes the Tommy.

MCNALLY STARTED BACK into his doorway, and then checked himself, and the delirium that had gripped him ceased to hold him, because the little sergeant and his boys were charging out of the doorway of the house, and there was a second or more when the Tommy gun wavered, undecided between McNally and the cops.

And then it didn't matter any more, because a half dozen bullets banged into the shrine, and one of them got Ling. The Tommy gun tumbled over the edge of the shrine and fell into the street, and a little puddle of water formed around it.

Ling was hanging over the edge of the shrine, and he was dead.

McNally began laughing. He laughed, and laughed,

because Ling was dead all right—but what had killed him stuck out between his shoulder blades. It was a knife, a cheap European knife such as the natives carried, and it had been thrown from behind. Only the handle showed.

Some native had had enough of Ling, and enough of waiting for the Regency government to send someone to get Ling, and that native had heaved a knife and killed the gangster. And gang rule in that little backwater district of Siam was broken, but it was not McNally and not the police who had done it.

McNally tried to think up something bright and chipper to say as he walked back into the house to the girl. Across the street, the Regency cops were pinching the local cops, a bunch of police together, settling their own difficulties.

But all McNally could think of saying was: "I was scared. I was so scared I nearly fainted. Would you—would you help me carry the cage to the boat?" The girl threw her arms around him.

… At six-fifteen the river boat pulled out, downstream. McNally had his cats installed in the main salon of the little stern-wheeler; he negotiated with the steward for a can of salmon, beamed as his musicians devoured the stuff.

Lisa stuck very close to him. Swell, cool, brave Lisa. He put an arm around her waist, and said, "Aren't they the little honeys?"

His arm tightened.

"Yes," she said. "They're darlings. I'd love to hear them sing. Do they really sing?" She looked at McNally fondly.

He'd never married because a wife was a poor thing to leave at home, and not many girls could be dragged around the world. But here was one that was used to it, that had been with her father on queer, dangerous Oriental adventures for years. And he wasn't getting any younger. It was very lonesome some of the places he went, she'd be a wonderful thing across a campfire....

"Do they sing?" he asked. "Do they sing? Say, if you could play that old harmonium there, they'd show you whether they could sing. Those cats'll be in the Met next season."

"I can't play the harmonium," Lisa said. "I can't play any musical instrument. Isn't that an awful way to be?"

A voice behind them said: "I'd be glad to play for you."

They turned. The woman who had spoken was older than Lisa, but still young. She said: "I'm Dr. Edwards, I've been up at the capital on some health work. Want me to play?"

McNally said: "Would you? Can you play *Sing Something Simple?*"

The doctor nodded. She went to the harmonium, struck a chord. McNally chuckled, and opened the cage, laughed outright as the cats listened to the music and made a bee line for the top of the harmonium.

Lisa listened to them sing, then said: "Dave." He didn't hear her. He was working out another tune for the doctor and the cats. She said: "Dave" again, and then smiled, a little sadly, a little amused, and went to her cabin to write a note to the boy in Peiping.